IDAHO

The meat allotments for the hungry Bannock Indians were late, and the tribe, never warlike or troublesome, had to leave their reservations to hunt for food. The army gathered its strength to find the Bannock and punish them. Gus Ruby, who knew about the army's terrible ruthlessness, joined with the Macdonald family to prevent another mass killing of Indians.

ARTHUR ST. GEORGE

IDAHO

Complete and Unabridged

LINFORD
Leicester

First published in Great Britain in 1993 by
Robert Hale Limited
London

First Linford Edition
published August 1994
by arrangement with
Robert Hale Limited
London

The right of Arthur St. George to be identified
as the author of this work has been asserted by
him in accordance with the
Copyright, Designs and Patents Act, 1988

British Library CIP Data

St. George, Arthur
    Idaho.—Large print ed.—
    Linford western library
    I. Title II. Series
    813.54 [F]

    ISBN 0–7089–7587–9

Published by
F. A. Thorpe (Publishing) Ltd.
Anstey, Leicestershire

Set by Words & Graphics Ltd.
Anstey, Leicestershire
Printed and bound in Great Britain by
T. J. Press (Padstow) Ltd., Padstow, Cornwall

This book is printed on acid-free paper

1

A Man with Two Sons

WHEN George Macdonald arrived in the country with half as many razor-back Longhorns as he had left Kansas with, it was called Colorado Territory and included Montana, part of Wyoming and all the area called Idaho. That was the year he rode out the worst drought he could recall. The same drought the Bannocks said they had no memory of in their word-of-mouth history, which went back hundreds of years before George Macdonald arrived.

Idaho Territory had broad rivers, huge lakes, rainfall that made things grow and snow-melt in its sequence of mountains which had fed the rivers and lakes since time immemorial.

There was considerable suffering.

George Macdonald came from the central Great Plains, he knew about droughts, knew the harbinger and took his cattle to the high country where they rode out the drought, gained weight on high country grass which had never been grazed over before. When he returned to his big valley ranch in the fall, a survivor where others had abandoned the land, he sold down to get cash to buy more land, and that became his hobby, buying grazing country, increasing his herd, ploughing his annual profit into more land.

By the time the territory became a state named Idaho, George had become as much a native as anyone except his neighbours, the Bannock and Nez Perce Indians.

By the time age had slowed him, his hair was white and his eyes were hidden behind squint-wrinkles, the land had filled up. Not as much as it had elsewhere. Idaho was never to grow as other areas did. For one thing stories of fierce

Idaho winters, troublesome Indians and lack of adequate communication between other parts of the country, discouraged settlers.

It would continue to discourage them long after George Macdonald was gone, but while he lived he was not really concerned about people. His holdings pretty well insulated him.

He took a Bannock woman to wife not long after arriving in the country. She was a tall woman with a wide forehead, an infectious smile, and lighter skin than people thought went with being an Indian.

She also worked beside her husband. George said later the best years of his life had been before she had died birthing their second child, another boy.

By the time she died George was well on the way to becoming independent and fairly well-off. After she died he concentrated more than ever on his holdings, his cattle, his two boys and horses. George had driven cattle from

Kansas but he had been born and raised to his teens in Texas. He had Texican manners, Texican outlook and temper. All his life George Macdonald had been careful not to give offence and was quick to take offence. He was never involved in the Nez Perce War of 1877, but he knew about war; he'd been orphaned by the War Between The States, had left Texas during the starve-out degradation imposed upon defeated Confederate States after the Civil War.

He knew about hunger and fear. He also knew the Nez Perce would never escape once the US Army went after the tribe.

Being right was no consolation. He and the Bannocks had been friends since George had arrived in their country. He wailed with them when the Nez Perces were beaten into submission after their Trail of Tears ended near the Canadian border where they sought sanctuary.

Their children had frozen to death,

4

the old Nez Perce starved, the women remained with their men to the last, riding half-dead scarecrow horses, never complaining, never allowing the soldiers to see their tears.

The very next year the Bannocks rose up because they were not allotted enough food despite the treaty which put them on a reservation, had promised otherwise.

Buffalo Horn, their leader, was killed by soldiers. Other Bannocks, seeking to find food, camas roots, were attacked by cattlemen and soldiers.

The Bannocks were humbled, their spirit was broken, George Macdonald hid as many as he could and defied the soldiers who rode into his yard with orders to hunt fugitives on his land.

He faced the army officer and his thirty dragoons with a rifle and six riders. He told the officer that the first soldier who hunted Indians on his land would be shot. The angry officer had accused George of sheltering hostiles. George's reply was blunt. "I don't know any hostile Indians. I know Indians who want to be left alone in their own country. Get your damned butt off my land and don't come back. If you do you won't get off as easy as you did with the In'ians. I'll give the newspapers something to write about all the way to Washington — a yard full of dead soldiers. Now *git*!"

The soldiers 'got' but a few days later another officer, this one accompanied by a staff, rode into the yard. George met them in the same way, only this time his riders were equal in number to the officer and his companions.

The officer was a full colonel. He was a burly man with a russet beard and pale blue eyes. When he moved to dismount George told him to stay up there. "In this country a man don't dismount in someone's yard unless he's invited to."

The colonel eased back in his saddle, slowly removed his smoke-tanned grey gauntlets and looked beyond George where his men were slouching with

Winchesters and sidearms.

He leaned aside and expectorated. Colonel Patrick Donavon was a tobacco chewer. He tucked the gloves under his belt and said, "Mister Macdonald do you know a man named Cluny?"

Macdonald nodded. "I know him. He's a pot hunter who peddles game around, mostly in town. What about him?"

"He told the provost you were hiding Bannocks."

Macdonald's face darkened. "He's been hunting on my land. I've told him ten times to stay off. He's a lying, underhanded son of a bitch. If you rode all the way out here — "

"Mister Macdonald, all I want from you is an answer, yes or no — are you hiding Bannocks?"

Macdonald hung fire. He detested liars right up there with thieves. "Colonel, what I do on my land is nobody's damned business."

The colonel's steady gaze remained. "You as well as told me you are hiding them when you said Cluny had been hunting on your range . . . Mister Macdonald, the army has authority to hunt Indians — anywhere. I think I should also tell you that hiding anyone wanted by the — "

Macdonald's temper was never far from the surface. When he interrupted the colonel his gaze was hard. "Mister, I don't know who made that law, but my land is deeded, I got full title, an' I never failed to settle up with trespassers. You turn around, take those lads of yours an' don't stop until you're out of my sight an' for five miles beyond because you'll still be on my range — an' you'll be trespassing. Now get!"

The colonel had met men like Macdonald many times before. He admired them for creating order out of the natural chaos of a primeval world. He had been faced down before too. He did a minimum of arguing, he did as he did now, he nodded without speaking, reined back the way he had come and rode away.

George Macdonald leaned aside his Winchester and called to one of the two youngest of his four man crew, who was his son Alfred. "Go find them In'ians, tell 'em we stalled the army for now, but they'll be back; they'll scour the mountains. Tell the In'ians to put watchers atop the bluffs so's the band can't be surprised, and keep as far from the soldiers as they can."

The youth turned, passed his brother and the other two riders to get a horse.

George spat, blew out a ragged breath and spoke to the men still standing around the barn with saddleguns. "They don't give up. One thing about the army I learnt long ago — when one bunch gets tired an' sets down, there's another bunch ready to do whatever they set out to do. You lads go on about your work; keep an eye open. If you see soldiers comin', skeedadle back here an' let me know. It won't be for a day or two, but they'll come.

Two riders turned toward a log shack to leave their carbines before going to the corral out back for saddle animals. The remaining rider, light-complexioned but with eyes as black as wet obsidian and hair to match, lingered long enough to say, "Paw, the whole country's full of soldiers. They'll come back with enough — "

"I know all that, Henry. But when they come back they won't find any Bannocks." Macdonald loosened, this lad was his favourite because of his two sons Henry alone reminded Macdonald of his mother. He smiled and spoke gently. "I can't stop 'em, an' I won't try. They'll find abandoned camps."

Macdonald shrugged. "They'll find tracks, they won't find any In'ians."

Henry gazed at his father without speaking. He was eighteen years old, old enough to have knowledge of the Nez Perce War and the Bannock uprising. He had been torn between two worlds, but Henry Macdonald did not believe his father's path was the right one. Everyone who got in the army's way ended up dead like his grandfather Buffalo Horn, or prisoners of an indifferent government and callous army.

He wanted to tell his father the Bannocks' trail had been ploughed under, there was no way to defy what had been emerging for at least ten years; what was clearly going to be the new path.

Macdonald said, "Just keep close watch, son," and turned away.

Henry leaned aside his Winchester and went out back for a horse. He had never smiled much, he did not smile now. He had visited the Bannock camp miles northeasterly in a broad expanse of forest, had seen the conditions of the Indians, had helped his father cut out two steers to be driven through the timber to the camp. On the ride back neither of them had said much. Henry hadn't really been able to identify with the fugitives, only to feel a depth of sadness over their condition.

George Macdonald, older, had known the Indians in their good era. He felt their displacement and suffering as though he had been one of them.

When they got home George was leaning on the tie-rack out front of the barn when his son finished caring for his horse and came out there. Macdonald had recognised something in Henry while he had still been very young; the same sensitivity his mother had possessed.

Alfred was different, more like his father, at times hard, always predictable, tough as a boiled owl, at twenty hard-fisted when the occasion arose, unwilling to yield when he thought he was right, slightly scornful of Henry who did not even like branding or altering, bloody, unpleasant things which could not be avoided.

Macdonald waited until his youngest was also leaning in warm sunshine before speaking. Aware of his youngest's sensitivity he had chosen and rehearsed what he had to say. Which was difficult because George Macdonald was a believer in being direct, bluntly straightforward.

"Suppose the In'ians hadn't been friendly when I first staked out this ranch, which was their land. Most likely I wouldn't be here now and neither would you. I treated them like friends, like equals. When they went through the Big Drought I drove cattle to their camps so they wouldn't starve. They warned me when hostiles was around. They helped me with the cattle before I could afford riders. Henry, what the army did was in my eyes, very wrong, an' I don't think they done it to the Bannocks by accident. They wanted to starve them. I tried to drive some cattle onto the reservation an' the soldiers turned me back. The soldiers knew the In'ians was starving. So, Henry, I couldn't help 'em when they revolted and took to the war trail. I knew they'd be whipped and herded back to their reservation like animals . . . You understand what I'm tellin' you? I owe them. Except for the damned army we'd all be living like things used to be. Your mother was a Bannock. They're as much your people as they are mine."

Henry said nothing, he looked dead ahead across the big yard to the rolling grassland beyond. Alfred, like his father, was stubbornly unyielding. If Henry told either of them what he thought, what he saw ahead, they would have very likely disowned him.

George studied the profile of his youngest. "I'm not afraid of the army," he said quietly. "The In'ians'll lead them through the mountains until their tongues are hanging out."

Henry turned slowly as he said, "For how long, Paw? How many Bannocks are there? How many soldiers are there?"

George had no trouble understanding the implication. His face reddened, his thin lips grew thinner. He too looked ahead out where meadowlarks were singing in the grass, where the immense sky of Idaho had a few puffy white clouds.

"I don't know," he said irritably. "No one knows, Henry."

"They know, the Nez Perces know. Paw, I know it's hard for them to admit defeat, but if they don't the army'll wipe them out."

"Not as long as there are mountains, son. The In'ians know the mountains better'n anyone."

Henry decided to offer one parting shot before walking away. He said, "Paw, I understand that you owe them. I know who my mother was. How long since they've been free people? I know reservation life is a grovelling experience — but what is the other choice? Maybe twenty, thirty years ago if they'd all banded together, but they didn't an' now it's too late. If they come in, if the army finds 'em in camp . . . "

Henry turned. "You haven't seen what it's like on that reservation. I

15

have. Any man worth his salt would rather be dead than live out his life in that kind of humiliation."

Henry straightened back off the tie-rack. "That's what they'll be, Paw. Dead. It's a different world than the one they knew. Maybe, for them anyway, it's a worse world, but ten, fifteen years from now, if there are any left, they'll understand things have changed. Changed forever."

George lingered out front as his son went back down through the barn. He stood a long time gazing far out and seeing nothing. Rarely had George Macdonald felt much interest in anything but building up his range and his herds. Fifteen years down the road . . .

He straightened up off the tie-rack heading for the main-house. Henry's mother, a wise woman, would probably have spoken to him today as her son had.

He went through to the kitchen, got his bottle from behind the wood box and swallowed twice before re-hiding the bottle, went to the parlour, sank down on the leather sofa and gazed at an oil portrait of his wife, and faintly smiled as he often did when gazing at her likeness.

She had been a perfect wife and mother. Rarely had George seen her angry, but the time he paid that itinerant sign painter six dollars to make the oil portrait, which was very good, she had exploded.

Six dollars was important to them when he'd done that. Now, she was gone and six dollars meant next to nothing, so George had been vindicated — only she was not around to know it.

2

Different Men,
Different Outlooks

SOMEONE had once said that any direction a man rode in Idaho was uphill, going or coming. For a fact Idaho was mountainous. There was no place in Idaho that mountains were not visible. George Macdonald was right in what he had said to Henry on two counts. One was that the Indians knew the area, the army would only see Indians if the Indians wanted to be seen. His second statement had been a prediction that the soldiers would ride themselves ragged and find no Indians.

But the army had Shoshone scouts so searching columns had little trouble tracking the Indians. The problem with tracking something, was that the tracker was always behind his prey.

After Alfred Macdonald found some tribesmen, gave them his father's message to be passed along, the companies of mounted soldiers did for a fact search, track, hunt and turn the air blue while wearing their horses down without finding a single Bannock.

Four times Colonel Donavon sent out details and four times they returned with the same report: No Indians sighted.

Patrick Donavon had been soldiering a long time. He had run tomahawks to earth from New Mexico's border country to Canada and back. He had been with General Miles when the Nez Perce had been stopped, had surrendered and had been driven south.

He had been successful against the Shoshoni of Colorado. It was his successes that put the eagles on his shoulders which, in his day, very few army officers wore who came up through the ranks.

Without leaving his log office at the improvised clutch of log structures around a large mustering area called Fort Taylor, after a barely literate general during the US-Mexican War, Colonel Donavon smoked a cigar and sat on a cocked-back chair gazing out the only window in his small office.

Donavon, the old campaigner, knew exactly what had happened. That old screwt named Macdonald had warned the Indians away. Among those armed men in the doorless wide opening of Macdonald's barn there had been a young 'breed, possibly Macdonald's son. Most of those pioneers spread their charm among the lodges and tepees.

Donavon had little trouble understanding Macdonald's sentiment. Donavon himself had watched the half-dead Nez Perce on their emaciated horses when the army cut them off from reaching sanctuary in Canada. He had not liked anything he had seen up there, possibly because of the stories his parents had told him of starvation and oppression in Ireland. More likely because Donavon had got a bellyful of tragedy and suffering during the Civil War.

He sat barely conscious of the noise in the yard, sounds of noisy horses, men yelling back and forth, a wagon's steel tyres grinding soil to dust.

When the cigar went dead he considered its gnawed butt and said, "Son of a bitch!" What he had to do — what his duty required him to do — was find those confounded Indians, corral them and herd them back onto their reservation, and he was convinced beyond a doubt that as long as that old cowman was around to watch Donavon's scouting parties and pass word to the Bannocks which way to ride to avoid being seen. Donavon had to either talk sense into Macdonald's head, or haul him back to the Fort Taylor brig.

The legality of the second alternative did not concern him. The army ruled.

There was not a lawyer within four, maybe five hundred miles, but even if there had been, the army administered Idaho, which was not a state but rather a territory, and would not become a state for a while yet. Not until mid-year 1890.

Donavon hunted up his adjutant, a red-headed, pale-eyed man, told him he was going alone to see Macdonald, and for his second-in-command to administer until he got back.

The adjutant whose most noticeable characteristic was a perpetually sun-burned nose, asked if the colonel hadn't ought to take an escort. "Them In'ians may be hidin' out but — "

"I'll go alone," Donavon said again, and struck out for the stabling area. Down there loafing troopers sprang up to do whatever was handy or, failing that, faded from sight out behind the stables.

Donavon and a corporal rigged out the colonel's animal. As he was riding westerly from the log buildings men stopped what they were doing to watch. By the time it was known where he was going, disapproval was not unanimous but even dissenters agreed he was either stupid or crazy to ride alone in full uniform when for all God knew, those damned elusive Indians had men watching the fort who would, if one went by past behaviour, catch the lone rider. Go after him quicker because he was in uniform. After the Nez Perce tragedy and the stunning defeat of the Bannocks, there would not be a friendly Indian within two hundred miles.

It was late spring or early summer, according to the way people interpreted changes in weather. It was pleasant riding weather, the sky was pale without a cloud, the land was carpeted with tiny flowers, and grass hip-pocket-high to a tall Indian.

The distance was considerable. Colonel Donavon did not expect to reach Macdonald's yard until late afternoon which, this time of year would still have sunshine.

He did not hurry. He let the animal pass along on a loose rein. He got a cud of molasses-cured tucked into his cheek, tipped his cap down to shield his eyes, and watched for movement the entire distance. He had no illusions about Macdonald's Indians. First it had been Custer over easterly, then Chief Joseph's people, after them the Bannocks.

It was beautiful country, with its everlasting mountains, its sparkling meadows, its variety of birds; no wonder the Indians felt dispossessed.

Colonel Donavon had been in Idaho a year. His orders had been to find a place to erect a fort and to simultaneously patrol the country, catch Indians where he could — not Shoshoni, they were friendly. Colonel Donavon and others like him used the Shoshoni as scouts and couriers. All other redskins found off reservations were to be apprehended or, if they fought, exterminated.

Government policy had not changed

one iota in twenty years and the army was the government's tool of enforcement.

By the time Donavon had Macdonald's buildings in sight he had been crossing Macdonald's land for many miles. He speculated about his reception. That old devil had left no doubt in Donavon's mind that he was as cold as ice, as hard as iron, and what folks back east who had never seen a free Indian, called an 'Indian lover'.

Macdonald probably was an Indian lover. If so, Colonel Donavon's reception might be cold at the least and openly hostile at worst.

He paused to swat at a mosquito, spat amber and straightened in the saddle for the last half mile.

Of course he had been seen and, close enough to be recognised by his uniform, they would be waiting.

And they were, Macdonald leaning on the tie-rack in front of his log barn, without a rifle this time but with a shellbelt and holstered sixgun, and beside him slouched another of those black-eyed, black haired men who looked enough like Macdonald to be the older man in his youth. Except the eyes, the hair, and something the colonel could not put his finger on.

Until he was in the yard he did not see anyone else but as he drew rein in front of the tie-rack, furtive movement showed inside the barn where sunshine never reached.

Donavon leaned to dismount and waited. Macdonald barely nodded. Donavon swung to the ground. The hard-faced younger man cleared his pipes and spat aside.

Donavon ignored that as well as the man who had done it. He had come to see Macdonald. He said, "I'd like to talk to you, if you've got the time."

Macdonald's answer was crisp. "I got the time."

"Without an audience if you don't mind, Mister Macdonald."

The older man straightened up slowly, jerked his head in the direction of the main-house and led the way to a covered porch that ran the full length of the building. As he gestured toward a chair with a rawhide seat, the cowman offered Colonel Donavon watered whiskey which the colonel politely declined.

Macdonald did not take a chair, he perched on the porch railing opposite his guest. Donavon had his earlier feelings about this meeting confirmed, Macdonald showed nothing but veiled hostility. The officer ignored the customary comments about the weather, the height of grass, local trade. He said, "Those In'ians are hard to catch, Mister Macdonald."

The other man nodded about that. "They've had to be for hundreds of years."

"I expect so, but they don't have eyes in the back of their heads."

"Meaning?"

Colonel Donavon's gaze strayed down across the yard, which was empty now. "Because someone's either helping them, maybe keeping watch for patrols and letting the In'ians know which way to go to avoid being seen, or is keeping them provided with meat and maybe fresh horses."

Macdonald made a derisive snort. "Since when have In'ians needed white men to supply them with meat or riding animals? As for the other, if none of us left this yard they'd see your patrols comin' from any one of a hundred rims."

Colonel Donavon was a man of considerable patience. He had learned that from the army where patience, sometimes called boredom, was only interrupted by action.

"Mister Macdonald, all the government wants to do is get the holdouts back on their reservations."

Macdonald made a bleak smile. "Is that all? Put them back where the army can watch them, starve them to death?"

Donavon knew about the Bannock uprising although he had not been actively involved. "I'd like to talk to their leaders. I'd like to explain that the allotment will be increased and — "

"Colonel, there was plenty of time to increase their allotment of food. Plenty of time. And you fellers knew they were starving. Do you know the figures for their allotment? *Two and a half cents per day per Indian!* If the army had to live on that, how long you figure it would be before soldiers would shoot some officers and take to the mountains? Colonel, I can't winter-feed one damned cow for that kind of money.

"Mister Macdonald, I just told you the allotment can be increased, once those holdouts move back to the reservation. I'll write Washington about — "

"An' what do they live on while you send a letter to Washington, it gets handed around, and finally the idea is put before Congress for action?"

Colonel Donavon changed his mind. He said he would like that watered whiskey if Mister Macdonald still wanted to offer it.

When he was alone in the shade of the overhang he loosened his coat, got rid of his cud and settled back. He was never in God's green world going to get cooperation from his host, which of course left his alternative, and that had to be thought out very carefully. He couldn't just ride into Macdonald's yard with soldiers and arrest the cowman. Sure as hell there would be a fight. Maybe Macdonald and some of his riders would get killed, but so might the colonel and his men, which would not be acceptable to the War Department, or the colonel.

When Macdonald came back with two tin cups half full and passed one to the officer, he resumed his perch on the railing as he said. "Why don't the army just leave 'em alone? They're not hurting anyone an' they can hide out in the mountains for years. Colonel, they've had a bad time, they've lost people, children, all they have left is cooking pots and a few horses. Even their ammunition has been reloaded so many times the casings are about half size which means they got to get close to kill game."

Donavon sipped his drink. He knew as well as he knew his name how he had to answer, and he also knew his answer was not going to go down with Macdonald. "Good whiskey," he said, holding the cup to his face.

For the first time George Macdonald almost smiled. "My father came from Scotland. He was a distiller by trade."

"You made this?"

"Yes. Been making a batch or two every year since I been out here . . . Colonel . . . ?"

"Mister Macdonald, I don't set policy and I don't have anything to do with how the army operates. My orders are to see that every In'ian who is off the reservation be put back there."

"Dead or alive?"

"Dead or alive. I know they can elude us. I also know something else.

Until they're on the reservation the army will not let up on them." Colonel Donavon rolled whiskey around in his mouth. It was the smoothest he'd ever tasted. His spirit soared a little, his face felt warm. "Something I can tell you personally. I was up north when the army blocked the Nez Perces from entering Canada. I doubt if there was a man in General Miles' detachment that liked what he was doing, but he had to do it . . . for me, it was a nightmare; babies too weak to cry for the milk their mothers didn't have, no old Indians, they had all died on the trek north. The animals were in terrible shape. It was enough to make a man sick."

"But you did it."

"Mister Macdonald, I take orders. Over years I've taken some that kept me from sleeping nights. But my job is to do what the government tells its general officers has to be done."

George Macdonald emptied his cup, carefully put it aside and gazed at the officer. "You've got a damned poor profession, Colonel. There's no law on earth can make me do what I know is wrong."

They sat a moment or two in silence. Colonel Donavon eventually broke it by arising to put his empty cup aside as he said, "I'd like to have a chance to talk to their head men."

"Wouldn't do any good, Colonel. You just told me what you had to do, an' I'll tell you what *they* have to do. Stay clear of the army if it takes ten, twenty years."

"The army will find them."

Macdonald smiled about that but spoke about something else. "My woman was a Bannock. My two sons are half Bannock. Right this minute, Colonel, I got to tell you I feel more Bannock than citizen of the United States."

"You won't arrange for me to meet their spokesmen?"

Macdonald wagged one foot and gazed at it before replying. "I'll tell you what I will do, Colonel. I'll tell their head men about our talk today. If they want to talk with you I'll bring them to my yard and send for you. But you come alone. If you figure later to maybe hide soldiers out yonder somewhere, they'll know an' so will I. An' they won't come."

Colonel Donavon knew this was the best he could get so he thanked Macdonald and started down off the porch toward the barn, and the moment he reached hard ground his legs wobbled.

Macdonald was with him and smiled. Colonel Donavon said. "Did you ever hear it said that In'ians and Irishmen can't handle whiskey?"

Macdonald laughed. He'd heard that said many times. Colonel Donavon laughed with him. At the barn a stone-faced rangeman brought out the colonel's horse, which had been stalled and grained, bridled and saddled the animal without a word, handed the reins to the officer without looking him in the face and sauntered out back.

Donavon eyed Macdonald. "It's nice to know you are admired for what you do in maintaining law and order."

Macdonald had a twinkle in his eyes when he replied. "I guess that's how a man looks at law and order."

Colonel Donavon led his horse outside, mounted and looked down at Macdonald. "When will you let me know if the In'ians will talk?"

"Depends on how long it takes to find them. Your scouting parties got them ducking and dodging. Maybe a week, maybe more. Don't worry, whichever they answer I'll let you know."

Donavon sat a moment considering George Macdonald, who could, the colonel knew, influence the Indians either way, and after their conversation on the porch he would have bet a good horse he knew which way Macdonald would slant his influence.

Well, he had done all he could do. It would be better for everyone if the damned Indians talked to him. He thanked Macdonald for his hospitality and rode out of the yard.

Alfred and that wizened, close-mouthed unsmiling rangeman appeared out front to join the older man in watching the colonel go back the way he had come. Alfred said. "How can a man stand that much hair on his face?"

His father ignored the question. "Where is your brother?"

"Out with Will."

"When he comes back tell him I want to see him."

" . . . Paw?"

"Alfred I got no answers. He wants to palaver with the head men."

"What's he got to offer?"

"Nothing the head men will like. Go back to the reservation and wait until someone a thousand miles from here agrees to increase the allotment."

Alfred turned toward the wizened rangeman. "If you see Henry before I do, tell him paw wants to see him."

The cowboy nodded and walked

away. He was one of those individuals upon whom sun and sleet, rain and wind had caused his skin to harden into something that resembled old leather left to the elements. He was lined and squinty-eyed, burnt the colour of saddle leather, a condition which was not unusual among men who spent most of their lives out of doors and who invariably looked ten, fifteen years older than they were.

His name was Arthur Headley. He too had been born in Texas and left as quickly as he could.

3

The Unshorn Stranger

HENRY and his father watched Alfred leave the yard with a bedroll aft of the cantle, with loaded saddlebags, riding a big, tough, savvy sorrel horse.

Henry said, "Maybe they'll come in, Paw."

Macdonald did not believe that for one minute. Why should they come in? They'd eluded the soldiers and could continue to do so. Mountainous country wasn't like open country.

In flat country a rider or a band of riders could be seen for miles. In mountainous country like Idaho, if someone had a reason to be elusive, they could avoid detection until hell froze over and for two days on the ice.

When his father remained silent Henry turned a little. "You don't think they'll come in?"

Macdonald continued to watch his oldest boy when he replied. "The colonel's not offering anything new." He looked at his youngest boy. "I wouldn't, would you?"

"If I didn't want to live like a fugitive the rest of my life I'd come in. Paw, no matter how long it takes, if the army don't catch them, someone else will. The land is getting settled. From what Art's told me, settler armies don't bring anyone back."

Macdonald finally lost sight of his eldest son. He said, "Henry, man was born to live free."

His youngest son said no more. It would have accomplished nothing. His father and his brother were as thick as oak; they had opinions and closed their minds to what was said that conflicted with those opinions.

Macdonald rode out with his riders to make a miles-deep encircling ride to find cattle. Henry did his part as he'd been doing it since he was eight years old. Checking for drift or 'down' animals, usually first-calf heifers, required little beyond being able to sit atop a horse.

Henry's father sent him easterly in the direction of thicket with several large fir trees in its centre. Over the years this particular, private place, had been used for calving cows. When the calving season was on, it was a fairly safe bet that some old momma cow would be calving in there.

Henry had to circle to his left to find the trail through the thicket. The brush was thorny, which seemed never to bother cows that were 'big' but it had always bothered Henry because a man astride caught every whipping limb that was higher than a cow's back.

The sun was almost directly overhead as he approached the trail. He was considering the thorny brush when he turned toward the patch, otherwise he might have noticed horse tracks.

The thorny trail was about three hundred feet long before the fir-tree clearing was reached. There was no brush in the clearing. In fact there was no grass either; the mat of fir needles prevented the growth of just about anything, as did the resin they had.

When Henry lowered his right forearm with the last stickery bush behind, he tipped his hat back, lowered his arm and met the head-on gaze of a rawboned man whose hair hadn't been sheared in a very long time, although the man had no face hair, which simply indicated that the man hadn't been near a tonsorial parlour in ages, but carried a razor in his saddlebags.

He was older than Henry, weathered and capable-looking. His horse, a muscled-up sorrel gazed at the intruders without making a sound.

The stranger smiled. Henry did not appear to be armed, except that a man never wanted to guess wrong about something like that.

The rawboned man nodded gravely

without speaking. Henry got clear of the brush, drew rein, leaned on the saddlehorn studying the stranger. He only nodded when he had finished the study. Whoever he was, the stranger wore run-down old scuffed boots, a faded butter-nut shirt, Mexican spurs, a shellbelt with a holstered Colt, and faded trousers.

His saddle, which was up-ended horn-down against one of the big trees, looked as hard-used as the man who owned it. The man spoke, finally, when it was clear Henry was not going to.

"Never thought anyone else knew where this place was. Only way I found it was watchin' a dog-wolf. He used the trail an' come back out. I thought he maybe figured a calvin' cow was in here." The man paused. "They kill baby calves when they can, but mostly they wait for the cow to take her baby away, then they get the afterbirth . . . My name's Gaston Ruby. It's not really Ruby, it's Rubidoux. Folks never pronounce it right and can't spell it, so I said my name was Ruby an' no one ever raised an eyebrow. No one ever called me Gaston, either. Just Gus. Gus Ruby . . . You got a name, young feller?"

"Henry Macdonald," Henry said as he eased into the clearing and swung to the ground.

"Glad to know you Henry. Was you expectin' to see a cow in here?"

"Maybe. Since I was eight years old I found 'em a few times."

Gus Ruby went back to his upended saddle and sat down. "Henry Macdonald . . . That's a decent name. Your folks own the land around here?"

"Yes. My paw's George Macdonald. We own the land for miles in every direction. My maw's dead an' I got an older brother named Alfred. You mind tellin' me where you come from, Mister Ruby?"

"Gus, just plain Gus. No, I don't mind. I come from the Fort Salish country up north an' west of here . . . It rains all the time in that country." Gus Ruby's eyes twinkled. "I had a notion that if I didn't get to dryer country my joints might get rusty. Tie up. Henry, set a spell. You're the first person I've run across in three days . . . Henry, you got any idea what day it is?"

To answer required thought. "Thursday, maybe?"

Gus Ruby laughed, it was a soft, deep, pleasant sound. "I'm not even sure what month it is," he grinned at Henry. "I haven't been in a town in months. Lots of nothin' in every direction where I come from. Mountains behind more mountains. Tell me somethin', Henry? What's the nearest town to where we're setting?"

"Clarksville, about four, five miles southeast."

Gus Ruby repeated the name. "Clarksville . . . They got a boarding-house down there? I'm gettin' wind puffs from sleepin' on the ground."

Henry described Clarksville. While he was talking the shaggy-headed man nodded. The description fit maybe a hundred towns he'd seen. "They got a telegraph down there?"

Henry shook his head. "The nearest town with a telegraph would be maybe Lewiston, about a hunnert miles from here."

Gus Ruby's next question was: "You was huntin' cattle — are there a ridin' job hereabouts?"

Henry could not answer this time. He knew all the stockmen roundabout, but had no idea whether they needed riders or not. "We don't," he said. "Paw already hired two a month or so back. I don't know about the other places."

Gus Ruby nodded. "It's a tad late to get hired on." He smiled again. "Maybe I'll just loaf this season. I been workin' too hard lately, anyway."

Henry, who had been schooled never to ask personal questions, took a chance. "You ride for a living, Mister Ruby?"

The older man regarded Henry

blandly. "Just Gus will do fine. Yes — well I been scoutin' for the army up north, but mostly I've worked for stockmen. Been at it man an' boy since I was younger'n you are. Henry, you got any tobacco?"

"No. I tried smokin' once and got so sick I never tried it again."

The older man regarded Henry with a sly look in his laughing eyes. "Well now, Henry. You can't be a quitter. You got to keep at it."

Henry smiled. "No thanks. Besides my paw'd most likely tan my hide."

"He don't smoke?"

"Not that I ever seen."

"Good man," Gus Ruby stated. "My grandmother used to tell me no gentleman ever blows smoke from his mouth, too unseemly. She taught me to dip snuff but I gave it up after she passed on and went to work to master smoking. That danged snuff made my eyes water all the time."

Henry had looked at the dozing, muscled up sorrel horse, dozing half in shade, half in sunshine. Henry knew a few things about horses; he could not have helped but know something about them. He said, "You got a good animal, Mister Ruby."

The rawboned man sighed. "Henry — just plain Gus — yes, he's a good animal, faster'n you'd think the way he's built. Five years old this year. We been partners since he was three." Gus Ruby assessed Henry's animal. "You're pretty well mounted too. What's that shoulder brand?"

"Walkin G M. Those are my paw's initials. George Macdonald."

Gus Ruby nodded. He had already observed that whoever had run the brand on Henry's animal was experienced; there were no blurred places from a too-hot iron applied too long.

Henry was poised to say something when Gus Ruby held up a hand for silence, arose soundlessly and gestured for Henry to stay where he was.

For a large man Gus Ruby moved like a cougar. He did not let a single thorny limb snap back as he moved through the underbrush on the trail until Henry could no longer see him.

Henry sat for what seemed hours to him before the rawboned man returned, resumed his place on the ground with the saddle supporting his back. He sat a moment in thought before facing Henry to ask another question. "What kind of In'ians you got hereabouts?"

"Well . . . some Shoshoni, some Bannock. Why?"

"A little band of 'em went past, looked to me to be about fifteen."

Henry was disturbed. Indians this far from the mountains would be seen, and he knew for a fact his father wouldn't like that because the army had scouts out.

He asked what they looked like. The older man described the ones who had been nearest to his place of concealment.

Henry said, "Bannocks."

"You got In'ians around here on the prod?"

Henry explained the local situation. While he was talking, he wondered about fifteen Indians being out in plain sight, if they were Bannocks. He had a chilling thought: If it was a war party, if the Bannocks had got tired of being hounded and had decided to carry trouble to the whites . . .

Gus Ruby read trouble in Henry's face. "You scairt of 'em?" he asked.

"My brother went to palaver with them this morning. What direction did they come from, could you tell?"

"I'd guess from the north west."

"My paw and our two riders were westerly lookin' for cattle in trouble."

"How far west, Henry, because my guess is that the bunch I saw came almost due south from up-country before slantin' away eastward." Before Henry could speak the older man went on speaking. "That damned fool Custer. After what happened to him, he got all the In'ians stirred up. A man used to be able to predict where In'ians would be. When it was time to

49

make meat, they'd be on their huntin' grounds. When the rivers was full, they be catchin' as many fish as they could to be smoked for winter. But now . . . Stay here, Henry, I'm goin' to see if they're still around or if there's any more. Henry . . . ? Don't let your horse nicker."

"What about your horse?"

"He won't make a sound, he was broke right."

Henry pondered that after the lanky man faded out along the thorny path again. How would a man go about training a horse not to nicker or whinny when he heard or smelled other horses?

Before the lanky man soundlessly appeared again, Henry had another question, but he did not voice this one, which was simply, why would a man train his horse not to nicker?

There was one plausible answer, Henry had just experienced it, a man would train a horse not to make a noise in hostile Indian country. But how? Horses weren't dogs, which learned

50

things fairly easily. A horse was not a dog. In fact just teaching a horse to carry a man was a real chore.

This time Gus Ruby did not return for almost an hour, which seemed like an eternity to Henry alone with two animals in their private place, surrounded by dense, tall stands of underbrush which made it impossible for him to see beyond his immediate location.

He listened. All he heard was brush-wrens busy as bees in the surrounding thicket.

The faded man returned looking sweaty. He sank down and smiled crookedly. "They're gone . . . I'd bet new money they're a raiding party. Maybe for horses, maybe for weapons, maybe to catch some folks out and slit their throats." He paused for a long moment before also saying. "Cheyenne. I've got reason to recognise Cheyenne when I see them."

Henry's frown appeared. "Cheyennes? They don't live in this country. Not that

I ever heard anyway. We got Bannocks an' Shoshoni . . . You certain they was Cheyenne?"

Gus Ruby put a narrowed gaze on Henry. "I know Cheyenne when I see them, Henry. They was Cheyenne. One time when I wasn't much older'n you I rode out of a steep canyon right smack-dab into a party of them, settin' their horses, goddied up with face paint an' all . . . I liked to have dropped dead. There was quite a bunch. I never counted 'em. I was fourteen at the time. They sat like they was carved of stone, not movin', not speakin', just settin' there. I was so scairt I hardly breathed. One of them, a real dark buck, rose up and flung his lance. I thought it was aimed at me. It was aimed to hit the ground a few feet in front of my horse . . . "

"And?"

" . . . And when I opened my eyes I'd fainted and fell off my horse."

"The Indians was gone?"

"Not right then. They sat watching

me, then the feller who owned that lance rode up, yanked it out of the ground and turned . . . They all started laughing. They was still laughin' when they rode westward along the foothills of them mountains I'd just rode out of. Henry I've seen lots of In'ians since that day. Mostly, I can recognise what kind they are, but for a fact I could spot a Cheyenne a mile off and I still can."

They left the hidden place together. Henry wanted to search for his father and brother. Gus Ruby offered no objection, but he was not the rather loose, languid man he had been at their meeting. Now, he would occasionally stand in his stirrups to look back.

Henry was impressed by the older man's attitude. He too had been frightened by Indians, but his fear had never lasted. Clearly, his companion's hair-raising at an early age had made an indelible and lasting impression.

It required two hours before they saw riders ahead. When they were closer Henry shouted. The riders halted and faced around. They had no difficulty recognising Henry, but they were sitting their horses blank-faced as Henry rode up with a stranger.

Henry blurted out what Ruby had seen. George Macdonald looked enquiringly at the rawboned, unshorn man. Ruby said the broncos had been Cheyenne. He did not do as he had done with Henry, he said nothing of how he had been certain, but evidently Henry's father did not question Ruby's identification, he simply said, "Might be a good time to head for home," and led off in a lope.

When they reached the yard and swung off to care for their mounts, Macdonald watched the lanky man. When the animals had been cared for he told his son and the riders to go clean up if they were of a mind to. As soon as they were gone Macdonald turned on the lanky stranger.

"I've never seen Cheyennes this far

west of their range, but others have. Was it a fightin' party?"

Gus Ruby nodded. "Looked like it to me. They was painted and they don't paint up usually until they have something in sight worth attacking. Then they paint up."

Macdonald stood a moment in thought. "Goin' east did you say?"

"Yep, easterly. What's over there? A town maybe, a big ranch that'd have horses?"

"The town's southward. They could change course, but I've never heard of In'ians attackin' a town in Idaho. If they try to raid Clarksville they better have more than fifteen broncos. Clarksville's a fair sized settlement. They'd boil out after In'ians like hornets."

Gus Ruby doubted that the Cheyennes would attack a town of any size. In fact he doubted that they would know there was a town where Clarksville was situated. But big cow outfits were something else. Cheyennes were some of the most skilled horse-thieves under the sun.

Macdonald took Ruby to the main-house, poured them both a drink and when Ruby asked about neighbours Macdonald shook his head. "Most outfits in this country set up their home place about in the centre of their range, which puts most of them awful far from one another for neighbours." Macdonald downed his drink, blew out a flammable breath and asked if the stranger would stay with his riders and son while he rode to town to spread the alarm.

The lanky man nodded. He set his cup aside, empty, and said he'd seen enough Cheyennes over the years to almost be able to distinguish them from other Indians by smell.

Macdonald returned to the yard with the stranger, eyed the position of the sun for some idea of how much daylight was left, pointed in the direction of the bunkhouse and continued on his way toward the barn to saddle up.

He was out front of the barn ready to mount when someone made a piercing whistle from a considerable distance. Macdonald tried to place where that sound had originated. While he was doing this a horseman coming toward the yard from the southeast was seen by someone in the bunkhouse. The men in there boiled out, each with a Winchester as well as a belt gun, except Henry, whose belt gun was hanging from a peg in the main-house. But Henry had someone's Winchester.

The riders crossed to where their employer was standing with the horse. They were looking for whoever had made that piercing noise. Wizened, leathery-faced Headley, raised a stiff arm. The others finally saw the rider, who was coming from the southwest in an easy lope. He was lost to sight when he rode past the main-house. He re-appeared again between the main-house and the log store-house.

It was Alfred Macdonald. He was riding straight up, the way men rode a horse with a rocking-chair lope.

He swerved between buildings and hauled down a walk in the direction of his father, his brother and the hired hands.

4

The Colonel's Quandary

THE colonel's eyes popped wide open when his orderly said the scouts had arrived, he said, "*Fifteen?*"

"Yes Sir, there's one that talks pretty good English out front. He told me the others are camped a mile or so from the fort in some timber."

Colonel Donavon dismissed the orderly, picked up his hat and went out front where a tall, swarthy man in stained buckskins arose to meet him. The colonel said, "Why'd you bring so many?"

The Indian, expecting a different greeting, spoke from an expressionless face. "We come through Shoshoni an' Crow country."

The colonel was not satisfied with

59

the answer even though he knew Northern Cheyenne were enemies of those other Indians. His problem was that Cheyenne had been with the Sioux at the Little Big Horn, and every man in his command knew it. He'd only sent for the Cheyenne because he knew they were the best Indian trackers west of the Missouri River. But — fifteen! No one in the colonel's territory, troopers or stockmen, would consider this many Northern Cheyenne as anything but an invitation for serious trouble.

He called to a passing soldier. "Find the lieutenant and tell him I want to see him."

While they waited the colonel motioned for the Indian to be seated, and took another chair. He'd expected army headquarters northeastward in Montana to send two, maybe three Cheyenne. If someone like old Macdonald knew fifteen Northern Cheyenne were at the fort, he'd send word to his Bannocks to ride hard, hide their families and animals, keep close watch and prepare to fight, which the Bannocks would most certainly do. Any Cheyenne, Northern or Southern, would be an enemy.

The colonel fished forth a dark looking cigar, offered it to the Indian, who refused, lighted up and blew smoke.

His idea had been to use enemies of the Bannocks to track them to their camp. The available Shoshoni had over the years been allies of the Bannocks. In fact there had been inter-marriage. He knew if it appeared the army might find the holdouts, some Shoshoni would either find the Bannocks and warn them, or pass the information to George Macdonald.

Gawddamit nothing was going right. He had a tentative deadline for finding those damned holdouts and getting them on their reservation!

When the junior officer arrived the colonel told him to take the Cheyenne with him, find out what the Indians needed in the way of supplies, get a wagon from the quartermaster and go with the Indian to the place where his companions were, deliver the supplies and come back. As the lieutenant was departing the colonel arose to address the Cheyenne, who also stood up.

"What's your name?" he asked.

"Ten Killer," the Indian said, then offered an acceptable English substitute. "Ten Hatchet."

"I'm Colonel Donavon. You can come to the post, but ride in alone. Keep your men in their camp. I didn't expect fifteen men, I expected two, maybe three. If the Bannocks and one particular cowman knows how many Cheyenne are scouting for the army, I'll have a war on my hands. You understand?"

Ten Hatchet looked faintly amused as he nodded. "Where was the last sign of the Bannocks you saw?" he asked.

Colonel Donavon gestured in a south-westerly direction. "In the mountains over there somewhere."

"How many Bannocks?"

Donavon scowled. "My best guess is maybe a hundred, maybe a few more. Women, old folks, children. Maybe thirty warriors . . . Ten Hatchet, all I want from you is to track them and find them. No fighting. Just find them and come back and tell me where they are."

Ten Hatchet finally did smile. "Colonel, we'll find them, but in this kind of country with peaks all around, when we come back and tell you where they are, and you march out in that direction, they'll see you and all you'll find is their old camp."

Donavon stood a long moment eyeing Ten Hatchet. The man did not learn English by picking it up. He had no accent at all and did not chop his words off. Donavon was curious about Ten Hatchet's background but said nothing. One Indian was not important, especially a Cheyenne.

He replied a trifle stiffly. "You find them, come back and let me know where they are."

After Ten Hatchet had departed to find the wagon of supplies, the colonel remained out front smoking for a long time, so long in fact that when a carroty-haired subordinate walked by, he looked twice. Donavon looked like a troubled man.

Later, after the wagon and the Cheyenne were gone, a sentry sang out that a lone horseman was approaching. By that time the colonel was back in his office.

There were a number of aggravating chores connected to being a post commander as well as his own adjutant. The ones Patrick Donavon liked the least were daily muster reports, daily information about supplies, the condition of horses, evidence of hostiles, and pay vouchers.

Those were the things he was hunched over his desk chewing an unlighted cigar and silently swearing about when the orderly appeared to say Mister Macdonald was out front, Donavon leaned back, fired up the cigar and told the orderly to send Mister Macdonald in.

George Macdonald had been in the saddle since before sunup and looked it. After they exchanged greetings Donavon sent his orderly for two mugs of coffee, got settled behind the desk and said, "Well?"

Macdonald slowly shook his head. "They said no. No meeting. They may be In'ians, Colonel, but they're not fools. They know what you want them to do and they aren't going to it. They're living better now than they ever did on the reservation."

Donavon slowly put the cigar aside and just as slowly leaned with both elbows on his desk before speaking. "You talked to them," he said, making a statement of it rather than a question.

George Macdonald shook his head. "Not personally, I didn't."

That scuttled what the colonel had been prepared to do the moment Macdonald agreed that he had spoken to the holdouts; have him locked up in the Fort Taylor brig.

They looked steadily at each other until the colonel leaned back off the desk to speak again. "Mister Macdonald, we can find them. We won't quit until we do. An' if they want a fight, we're prepared to do that too ... As for finding them, Mister Macdonald, it won't be as hard as you and they think." Donavon paused ... when he spoke again he had changed the sound of his voice.

"You have to know we'll find them. No matter how long it takes or how far we have to go, so, why not explain their position to them. I don't want a war. That's the last thing I want ... Wear down men, wear out horses, campaign until the snow flies."

George Macdonald sat expressionless through the officer's harangue, then stood up to depart as he said. "We got different ideas about you findin' them, Colonel. But in any case, they don't want to talk to you ... Maybe if you'd agree to supply the reservation first, an' they saw you do it, maybe they'd at least council with you. Maybe; I'm just guessing."

Donavon's patience ended. As he stood up he said, "You're in communication with them and I can — "

"Am I, colonel?"

Donavon reddened. "You're gettin' in over your head, Mister Macdonald. When we corral them there'll be someone who will confirm for us that you been helping them . . . All I need is one tomahawk to verify that, an' I'll have you in my brig where you'll sit until you're a lot older than you are now."

George Macdonald's temper was also up. He looked squarely at Patrick Donavon and said, "If there's trouble, colonel, take my word for it, the feller with whiskers dressed like an officer will be one of the first killed."

After the cowman's departure Colonel Donavon hunted up his quartermaster, a thick-necked old campaigner whose salute was never more than casual. He had served under some of the best of them years back. Grant, Sheridan, Sedgewick, Sherman. He had one of the few decorations men won during the Civil War, a bronze star.

He had arisen from a shaded bench when he had seen the colonel approaching. He leaned to knock dottle from a foul little pipe and wait.

Donavon's first words were: "Did the wagon go out with supplies?"

The old campaigner looked at Donavon from beneath thick brows. "Yes sir, it did. Ought to be back shortly. Colonel . . . ?"

"Yes."

"If that In'ian on the seat with the lieutenant was guidin' the course of the wagon . . . Sir, we loaded enough supplies into that wagon for more'n a scoutin' party."

Colonel Donavon stepped into shade and sat down. The old campaigner knew his place. He also knew Patrick Donavon had come up through the ranks, but he continued to stand in

68

the presence of a senior officer until Donavon told him to be seated, which the quartermaster did with a grunt, sitting on the same bench but at the opposite end of it.

Donavon told the old campaigner where the wagon had gone and why so many supplies had been taken out there. The scarred, slovenly older man leaned back as he said, "Can't you send all but three back where they come from — Sir?"

"I could," the officer replied, then explained about George Macdonald and what the colonel was positive Macdonald was doing — keeping the Bannocks informed about the soldiers. The bulky, scarred man leaned forward and fixed perpetually squinted eyes on nothing but far out as he quietly said, "So you figure you might need all them Cheyennes."

Donavon would not admit this was his reason for being willing to keep the Cheyennes, despite what he knew would happen if Macdonald or the

Bannocks knew the Cheyennes were in their territory. He said, "They're the best sign-readers, Sergeant."

The older man replied dryly. "And hard fighters as Colonel Custer found out . . . Sir, supposin' the Bannocks learn that their hereditary enemies is with us at the fort?"

"If things work out," Donavon replied. "If we can find the Bannocks before Macdonald and his In'ians know the Cheyennes are here, maybe we can end this damned mess before hot weather arrives."

After the colonel headed back to his office the old campaigner re-lighted his pipe, watched Donavon until he was no longer in sight, and slumped in shade.

Pat Donavon should know that the quartermaster was not the only one on the post who saw the wagon leaving the compound with an Indian on the seat with the driver.

Maybe Donavon had forgotten, but some of the best guessers, observers and gossips on earth were soldiers pulling garrison duty.

Two days later Donavon took four men and rode west, in the direction of the countryside which offered easiest access to the rugged mountains.

He was crossing Macdonald land.

He rode up a sidehill, where he and his companions were less than a hundred yards where a lanky, un-shorn rangeman was picking a stone out of the hoof of a muscled up sorrel horse.

They exchanged a long look, both the colonel and the lanky man clearly surprised.

The bony-shouldered man dropped the hoof, broke out a smile and called a greeting. "Howdy, gents. I didn't know there was any soldiers around here. But then maybe I wouldn't anyway. I just been in this territory a few days."

Colonel Donavon led the way down the slope to where the lanky man was standing beside his horse. The officer asked the man his name.

71

"Gus Ruby. What's yours?"

"Colonel Donavon. What're you doing out here?"

"Well sir, I been stayin' with the Macdonalds until my horse rests up a little."

The sorrel horse looked to Pat Donavon as though he was in perfect condition. The colonel leaned on his saddle-swell where the horn would have been if he hadn't been straddling a McClellen. "You're a friend of the Macdonalds are you, Mister Ruby?"

"Well since I been stayin' at their place I guess you could say I am . . . Why? You got somethin' against them?"

Donavon reddened. The man standing nearby was unkempt, badly in need of a shearing. His clothes were disreputable. He looked to Pat Donavon like a saddle tramp. Because of that, and from habit, he did not like civilians of any kind shooting questions back when he answered Donavon's questions. The officer formed an opinion. If Gus Ruby

72

wan't a red-necked former Confederate Pat Donavon would be horn-swaggled. Ruby knew he was addressing a Union officer. He kept smiling and stinging the colonel with the kind of insubordination former Rebels commonly employed.

Donavon asked if Ruby had seen any riders. The rawboned man continued to smile as he shook his head. "Just a few head of cattle an' some horses." Ruby put his head slightly to one side, continued to smile up at the officer and asked if Donavon meant had he seen any Indians, in which case he said, he hadn't, and did not believe this was the kind of country Indians liked a whole lot.

Colonel Donavon raised his left hand with the reins in it, jerked his head and rode off. Gus Ruby watched the blue uniforms until they were small in the distance, then turned toward the brushy end of his arroyo and quietly said, "Alfred, they're long gone . . . But I can tell you one thing for a fact. That colonel looked surprised as

hell when he topped out up yonder."
Gus laughed. "I tried to look just as
surprised."

Alfred Macdonald came out of the
underbrush. Under the circumstances he
probably should have looked pleased,
instead his black gaze was fixed on the
ant-size party of soldiers as he said.
"Good thing Paw wasn't here," and
turned back without explaining what he
meant. After a few minutes he emerged
from the thicket astride a horse.

This time he smiled at the man on
the ground. "You got him about half
mad, Gus."

"I got reason not to be fond of them,
Alfred. Now I expect one of us better
get back to the yard an' tell your paw
there's soldiers around."

Alfred was agreeable. "You go, Gus.
I got to palaver with the hideouts again.
See you tomorrow."

Gus leaned across the seat of his
saddle watching young Macdonald lope
northwesterly.

By the time Gus got back to the

yard Henry and the other two riders, Arthur Headley and Will Stratton, were already through for the day.

Gus cared for his sorrel horse, crossed to the main-house, told George Macdonald what had happened, and saw colour mount into the older man's face.

Macdonald was scowling when he asked which way the soldiers had gone. Gus gestured southward. "For as long as I could see, they never turned off."

Gus went down to the log bunkhouse where Art Headley was working at the stove. Henry listened to what the lanky man had to say, left in a hurry to go find his father.

The last few days Henry had been having some pretty nightmarish premonitions which he kept to himself. He wouldn't have told the hired hands, and he certainly would say nothing to his father.

After supper Will, Art and Gus went out front where Gus played a mouth harp. Art and Will were impressed, rightly so, Gus was as good a player as they had ever heard. He played several songs and kept returning to one particular song. It was entitled *Lorena* and had been popular with Confederate soldiers during the Civil War.

Eventually the yard was empty and the lamps had been doused. Some coyotes sounded while on the run. It sounded like a fair-sized band of them.

A corralled horse snorted; most horses were not upset by night-roaming coyotes. But if one had ever been chased, or surrounded and had fought clear, every time he heard their sounding as long as he lived, he scuffed dirt, flung his head up and snorted.

It was a bland night, cloudless, faintly fragrant from rangeland flowers, all small, all seasonal, and all shyly fragrant.

When dawn arrived the riders and Henry had eaten, cleaned up and were ready to resume their coursing across Macdonald range looking at cattle.

There was some wariness among them about riding near thick stands of brush or where trees cast shadows. Henry knew the Bannocks and was not the least worried, but Stratton and Headley were older men, they were well aware of the consequences of riding into an ambush.

Stratton paused once to point. Two riders were speeding southeastward side by side and clearly in a hurry. If they saw the Macdonald riders they gave no indication of it. Possibly whatever they were up to prevented them from watching for other horsemen.

Art Headley's brow creased, his sunk-set narrowed eyes were thoughtful. "Want a guess, fellers?" He asked and did not await an answer. "Them was In'ians an' sure as I'm settin' here they wasn't Bannocks."

5

A Maze of Mountains

THREE days after the arrival of the Cheyenne at Fort Taylor that lanky, easy-smiling stranger returned from a day-long ride, cared for his animal and with dusk settling, strolled toward a lighted lamp in the kitchen of the main-house.

George Macdonald, whose feelings toward the un-shorn man were ambiguous, met him at the doorway and nodded. Gus Ruby smiled. "Mister Macdonald, you got any Cheyenne In'ians in your territory?"

George gazed steadily at the tall man with a faint frown forming. "Cheyennes? I never heard of any this far from their home country."

"Well, I was nosin' along in that timbered country west of here an' come onto three sets of barefoot horse tracks. Bein' curious I left my horse hid, climbed one of them pointy hills an' set up there in some pine trees; just set there. It was pleasant, no direct sunlight. The view was of a lot of mountainous country west an' south."

Macdonald was not a patient man, but this time he had to be. About the only thing he had learned about the rawboned man was that he would not be hurried.

"It took a while," Ruby said. "I figured, since the tracks went up in there, In'ians was most likely still in there. They was; with the sun slantin' away I seen 'em twice, once when they met afoot, the second time when they was ridin' back down out of there, an' you can take my word for it — I got reason to recognise Cheyenne when I see 'em. They went down-country west of my hill, kept on riding."

Macdonald's frown lingered. "Any chance you was wrong?" he asked.

"No sir. Like I said, I got reason to know Cheyenne when I see 'em. Somethin' you could likely tell me; what's northeast of here?"

"Fort Taylor, where that colonel commands."

Ruby considered that for a while before speaking again. "You don't expect the colonel sent for 'em, do you?"

Macdonald's answer was curt. "I don't know about that, but if they was into the mountains west of here, I'll guess they were huntin' Bannocks."

Ruby nodded slowly. "They got a reputation of being the best In'ian trackers around. If your Bannocks was within range of where they was snoopin', I'd say they found them. And since they was ridin' toward that fort, a man'd just about have to suspect they was scoutin' up Bannocks for the army."

Macdonald eyed the lanky man. He did not look clever and did not act clever, but right there on the porch with dusk settling, Macdonald decided that, whatever he was, Gus Ruby could be a good man to have around — for a while anyway.

After Gus Ruby left, George Macdonald sat on his porch with night settling and light showing from the only small window in the bunkhouse. He would have enjoyed Henry's company, the main-house was empty without his wife. Alfred lived in the main-house but since Henry had become a regular hand, he preferred to live at the bunkhouse.

If the grinning tall man was shrewd, George Macdonald was equally as shrewd and, under the present circumstances, because he knew more of what was happening, he could more readily fit bits and pieces together.

For example, he recalled the colonel's words the last time they met. "As for finding them, Mister Macdonald, it won't be as hard as you and they think."

Cheyenne might be good trackers

81

and sign-readers, but they did not know the mountainous country which covered seemingly endless miles in three directions. George decided to send Alfred to tell them what his father suspected the army was up to, and to suggest that, along with keeping watchers atop vantage points, they strike camp and go west, keep going west and leaving many false trails, until they were so distant, even if the Cheyenne found them, they would be too far for the army to follow twisting, dangerous canyons in pursuit.

It was not a foolproof idea, but until Macdonald had slept on it, it would suffice. He knew that whatever else would happen, this would in all probability be the end of the Bannock problem once and for all. Either they escaped — and they were also very good at reading sign and deluding pursuers — or they were run down, but whichever way it ended would be the way things would be for the Bannock for many, many years.

Macdonald was not the only one who lay awake in the darkness. Gus Ruby had both arms under his head as he pondered. Bannock Indians did not mean anything to him one way or another and, to not quite the same degree, neither did George Macdonald, but he had leaned toward his viewpoint accepting his hospitality and more to the point — Gus Ruby hated blue uniforms.

In the morning Macdonald told Alfred over breakfast what he wanted done. His eldest son was agreeable. He made up two bundles, one for each of his saddlebags, said nothing to anyone as he saddled a horse, and left the yard riding southwest, although he knew that course would not take him directly to the Bannock camp.

Macdonald looked for Gus Ruby, did not find him, had his riders make a search which was also unproductive, so Macdonald left the yard with Henry, Will and Art, a little troubled — he had never felt that he knew Ruby. Of course the lanky man had reported strange Indians in the area, but he could still be either doing something secret on his own, or he could be a spy for Colonel Donavon.

Macdonald did not smile all day.

He might have looked even more morose if he could have seen Ruby on his powerfully put together sorrel horse dogging Alfred's tracks with obvious prudence and probably considerable experience at shagging folks.

Alfred looked back occasionally, he stopped dead-still to listen at other times, and each time he did this Gus Ruby seemed to have anticipated it. The up-ended country behind Alfred Macdonald was empty.

The sun climbed. It was hot on the rims, the plateaus and the ridges, but among the canyons where daylight only briefly shone at midday, where there were trees, thornpin thickets, occasionally sluggish little creeks, and huge boulders which had fallen from high above to completely block some of the canyons. In these places animals had done what came naturally to them. Tramped new trails up and around the blockages.

The farther Alfred and his shadow went, the more rugged the terrain became. Twice Gus Ruby saw horse tracks which young Macdonald evidently did not see because he rode across them without even hesitating. Gus assumed those tracks had been made by the Cheyenne the day before, and it troubled him to think the Cheyenne had penetrated so far into the wild mountainous country.

Depending how much farther Alfred had to go to meet the Bannock, Gus hoped the Cheyenne had turned back before they got close enough to smell smoke or hear noise from the Bannock encampment.

His hoping conjecture was correct although he did not immediately know it. What he *did* eventually know was the place where the Cheyenne had turned back, probably so as not to be caught in this wild place after dark.

Gus halted in a tangle of willows beside a cold-water creek to rest his horse, allow it to drink, while he considered land-forms. He suspected that Alfred was on the last leg of his journey. Gus would have liked to have a smoke, but scent of any kind carried far in air as pure and scentless as the air was in the mountains.

His horse suddenly threw up its head to scan a forested slope. Gus traced out the area the horse was watching — and saw Indians.

They may have been atop a vantage point, had seen and recognised Alfred, and had been watching the shadowy man on the sorrel horse who had been following young Macdonald.

Gus freed the tie-down over his holstered Colt, leaned across his saddle watching for another sighting among the big trees, and something poked him gently over the kidneys from behind.

He did not move.

His sixgun was lifted away. For a

time there was no sound, nothing he could see without facing about which he did not do.

A guttural voice spoke softly. When Gus remained fixed and motionless a powerful set of fingers gouged into his shoulder forcing him around.

The Indian facing him was close to Gus's height and build. He could even have been about Gus's age although that would forever have to be speculation. The whites of his eyes were muddy-coloured. He had a skinning knife on a bullet belt. His sixgun was old, one of the cap and ball variety. He held Gus's later model Colt in his fist as he made a slight trilling sound.

Gus felt like swearing. While he'd been watching for Bannocks up the westerly sidehill, a second party had crept up behind him. They had even fooled his horse which was still looking up the opposite slope.

Gus needed no explanation. While he had been following young Macdonald, the Indians had seen him from some high place and had hurried to get between Gus Ruby and Alfred Macdonald.

Gus sighed, considered the Indians, all stalwart business-like individuals armed with an assortment of weapons. He shook his head in the direction of the man facing him, fished forth his makings and as the Indians from the west slope hurried down, Gus rolled and lighted a smoke under the eyes of the Indians facing him.

As he blew out his first inhalation he asked the Indian who had caught and disarmed him, if he could speak English. The Indian nodded and asked a question of his own. "Who are you? Why are you following the other rider?"

Gus trickled smoke and smiled a little. He knew nothing about Bannocks, had never seen one that he knew of before this afternoon, but he was perfectly willing to admit they were anything but bug and root eaters or, if they ate those things like the

Diggers down south, at least they were not dense.

Instead of answering the Indian's questions Gus said, "How far back did you see me?"

An older man, scarred, with venomous eyes and a slit of a mouth, spoke harshly. The English-speaking Indian listened but did not look around at the speaker. He said something back in the same strange language, then held up a little sharpened stick, and smiled. It was this harmless toy he had pricked Gus in the back with. He tossed the stick aside and repeated his earlier question. "Why are you following the other rider?"

Gus's lazy grin widened. "You mean young Macdonald?"

Not a one of the Indians showed anything but impassivity. Gus decided to give up playing games. He said, "I was following him to make sure he reached the Bannock rancheria . . . Were you keeping watch yesterday?" Before an Indian could reply Gus's smile lingered as he said. "If you was you must have fallen asleep. There was Cheyenne searching the mountains for your camp."

The Indian looked as surprised as Alfred's father had looked. "Cheyenne don't live in this country. This is Bannock country. Cheyenne live many — "

Gus broke in to say, "I know where the Cheyenne live. I got reason to know about them. Whatever-your-name-is, take my word for it. Yesterday there was Cheyenne up in here lookin' for your camp. That's what young Macdonald rode all this way to tell you today."

The Indians spoke swiftly among themselves, but briefly. The bronco who had taken Gus's sixgun faced him and gestured. "Get on your horse and follow us . . . If you want to see sunup in the morning . . . " The Indian cocked and uncocked Gus's sixgun.

The trail was longer than Gus had thought it would be, but at least when they went out of one canyon by way of a prehistoric wash-out and into a different canyon, their new trail was at the bottom of a much wider canyon with abundant feed and browse as well as another stream which ran against the opposite sidehill from the one the Indians used.

Without Gus realising it because he was facing ahead, other Indians joined the little party from both sides of the new canyon they were traversing. Not until he smelled cooking fires and tried to guess about where the sun had slanted off to, and twisted in the saddle to attempt that, did he see that the little party which had left the capture-site with him, had roughly doubled. He sat forward beginning to believe the Bannock just might be as *coyote* as the Cheyenne.

Two broncos left the party in a trot. They were lost to sight around a bend in the canyon, but Gus guessed where they had gone and why, to let the encampment up ahead know they were bringing a prisoner with them.

Gus leaned to watch when a slight curve again obscured his view. But the bend continued to tease him for nearly ten yards, then the trail straightened and he pursed his lips to a silent whistle, not at the size of the rancheria but surely, since Alfred had already preceded Gus with his message to abandon this idyllic place and run for it, the Indians who were concentrating on their fires and other camp chores as though they did not have a worry in the world.

6

The Scent of Trouble

ALFRED MACDONALD was in a conical brush shelter with several older men when the noisy arrival of Indians with a white man amongst them brought Alfred to the door of the hut. He stood gazing as Gus went by. Ruby acknowledged Alfred's gaze with a smile and a shrug.

The Bannock who claimed honour for capturing the rangeman herded him past impassive villagers to the hut where Alfred was standing, handed Alfred Gus's sixgun and walked away.

Gus said, "It'd be pretty hard for even Cheyenne to sneak up on these folks."

Alfred had a disposition like his father, but being younger he was less inclined to restrain it. His glare was fierce as he said, "Did you shag me?"

Gus nodded, this time without smiling. "Yep. Maybe you don't know Cheyenne, but I do. There's no better trackers in the world. I wanted to make damned sure you got where you were going."

Alfred seemed not to be mollified. He said. "The Bannocks got sentries on just about every high place for miles. They seen no Cheyenne, no one at all until they seen you shagging me."

Gus considered the angry younger man. "I know the Cheyenne. I ain't surprised your Bannocks didn't see them, but believe me, they scouted up these hills." At the look he was getting from young Macdonald he slowly wagged his head. "I know the Cheyenne. Your In'ians wouldn't see them if they didn't want to be seen." Gus gestured. "They got mountains all around. There's been Cheyenne scoutin' up this canyon." Gus dropped his arm.

Alfred remained stone-faced. "An' I suppose you got past them?"

"No. I didn't see any new sign. My guess is that they went back to whoever they're workin' for. The army maybe."

Young Macdonald let his gaze wander around the large camp and back before he spoke again. "I'll ask them to scout. Maybe the Cheyenne are good, but they leave signs just like anyone else . . . Anythin' else you want up in here?"

There wasn't. "Maybe somethin' to eat."

Alfred turned as he jerked his head. Gus followed him into a dark council lodge where four older men eyed Gus impassively. They sat like stones as Alfred told them what the stranger had seen. Without a word two of the older men arose and went outside. The other two remained seated. Alfred motioned for Gus Ruby to sit down, which he did, then Alfred spoke to the Bannocks in their own language.

95

The Indians ignored Gus. After a flurry of conversation the remaining two Bannocks departed.

Alfred faced Gus across a mound of ash surrounded by stones. They'd had little contact up until now. Alfred asked a question. His manner was direct. "Why did you shag me?"

"Because I knew the Cheyenne were around, an' I also knew you folks been helpin' these In'ians. It's none of my business, but as long as I'm eatin' your paw's grub, I owe him this much." Gus leaned slightly with both elbows on his knees. Now, he was not smiling. "I don't know your tomahawks but I *do* know the Cheyenne. Any time fifteen go somewhere together, without squaws or pups, someone is goin' to dig graves. If you can get these In'ians to run for it, you better explain to 'em the only way they can escape Cheyenne trackers is to sprout wings."

"Or set up an ambush," Alfred replied dryly. "They know the mountains."

Gus continued to sit forward another

moment or two, then leaned back. "Partner, these an' the Sioux are the people who took care of the Seventh Cavalry, an' the cavalry had Crow scouts with 'em."

Alfred picked up a half-burned twig and stirred ash with it as he spoke. "These folks will take care. It's not them I wonder about." He stopped stirring and raised black eyes to Ruby.

Gus smiled. "I'll tell you what I told your brother. I got tired of rain every day or two up north where I worked for the army, so I drifted south. When I leave your country I'm goin' to keep goin' south. Like I already told you, a man that feeds at another man's trough, owes him."

Alfred tossed the twig among the ash and arose. "You can go back any time you want to. But it might be a good idea for you to stay away from Fort Taylor. If you go visitin' over there . . . The trees got eyes."

Alfred left the dark brush shelter followed by Gus Ruby. They had to hesitate briefly to allow their eyes to adjust to bright sunshine. Alfred jutted his jaw in the direction of some cooking pots. "Help yourself," he said, and went in search of the older men who had been in the council house earlier.

Indians eyed Ruby, not always directly — it was bad manners to stare — but they watched him approach a perspiring dark woman, wrinkle his nose over the aroma of her pot and look enquiringly at her. The woman, ugly as original sin, filled a wooden bowl and handed it to Ruby without a sound, and continued her stirring after he had found a place to sit and eat.

When he returned and held out the bowl to be refilled, the woman broke into a wide smile and refilled the bowl. She said something to another older woman nearby. They both laughed.

Alfred Macdonald came into the shade where Gus was eating, hunkered and said, "Are you going back to the ranch?"

Gus nodded while chewing tough but

flavourable meat.

"Did my paw know you were goin' to shag me?"

Gus put a slightly disgusted look on the younger man, and continued to chew.

Alfred accepted the look as an answer and asked another question. "You lived with the Cheyenne?"

This time Gus paused between mouthfuls, and told Alfred the same story he had told Henry.

Alfred lingered briefly before leaving. Gus watched him. He went over where two big Indians were standing to talk to them.

Gus wiped his chin on his bandana, wiped his fingers on his trousers, rolled and lighted a smoke which lasted until he had seen as much of the rancheria as he wanted to see, then went to find his horse.

Two youths were letting the sorrel pick grass with a rawhide lariat around his neck. When Gus appeared one of them departed, the other one smiled.

Gus dug in a pocket, found a silver coin and handed it to the lad. He then bridled his animal first, before slipping the rawhide rope off, then put the saddle back on which the Indians had removed. He swung up, turned and without another glance back, rode back the same way he had arrived.

Finally, it was hot in the canyons, but less from overhead sunshine than from heat it had put down into the canyons before sliding out of sight to the west.

Gus found the wash-out between two canyons, crossed back into the narrower canyon and slouched along until he encountered one of those long-spending curves. There, he rode up behind some flourishing underbrush, dismounted and waited.

The mounted Bannock came along as Gus had expected. He only occasionally glanced at the ground for tracks. There was no need in most of the canyons because there were very few places where four-legged or two legged critters could climb out. Once in most of those canyons a man or an animal had to keep going in one direction or the other.

Gus squatted, rolled and lighted a smoke, and waited. When the Indian appeared he was slouching, indifferently watching the trail ahead — and made a mistake. Because he had been on Gus's trail since shortly after Ruby departed from the rancheria, and because he knew this canyon as well as most other canyons, he assumed the whiteman was on ahead.

Gus let him pass, killed his smoke, led his horse back to the trail, mounted and rode around the bend — where the Bannock was sitting his horse smirking. Gus's ruse had backfired. As they faced each other the Indian made the motions of someone smoking.

Gus was humiliated but not a whole lot. He grinned, the Bannock grinned back, Gus continued down-canyon, the Indian rode back the way he had come.

Arriving back where sunshine shone

in all directions, Gus aimed for the Macdonald yard, which he reached with dusk on the way. George and his riders had already returned, cared for their animals and left the barn, but as Gus was off-saddling a quiet, hard voice spoke from behind him.

"We missed you."

Gus looked over his shoulder to where George Macdonald was standing just inside the front barn opening. He went back to caring for the sorrel as Macdonald said, "You shagged Alfred?"

Gus was slow answering. "Well, we met, but the Bannocks found me first and herded me along to where I met Alfred at their rancheria."

Macdonald showed no expression as he said, "Why did you shag him?"

"To tell him about the Cheyennes."

"I'd already told him."

"And to tell him the Cheyenne were the best sign-readers in the world, and they'd scouted up some of those canyons, an' whether he believed me

102

or not, fifteen Cheyenne amounted to a war party an' for him to get the Bannocks to scatter an' watch their back-trail."

George Macdonald walked closer to sit on an up-ended horseshoe keg. Ruby had said things George had not told Alfred, but they were simply details. George said, "They got quite a camp, don't they?"

"Yes, and they keep good watch from high places — but Mister Macdonald, I don't figure you know the Northern Cheyenne real well. If you did, I wouldn't have rode into their camp where they was cookin', lyin' around, acting as though they didn't have a care."

"Alfred went up there to warn them."

Gus turned with the shank in his hand ready to take his horse out back and release it. "I got a feelin' that don't you or your lads or them Bannocks got any idea what they'll be up against if they don't disappear in small bands.

Cheyenne can read sign where there ain't any. Fifteen of them ridin' with soldiers . . . " Gus turned to lead his horse out back. When he returned George Macdonald was gone.

The following afternoon Colonel Donavon appeared in the yard when everyone except Gus Ruby was gone. They had rigged out before daybreak.

The colonel dismounted near the wagon shed where Gus was standing. He enquired about the Macdonalds. When Gus explained that they were somewhere on the range and had left the yard close to sunrise, an Indian mounted on a spotted-rumped horse barely smiled. Gus read that faint expression correctly. Colonel Donavon knew Gus was the only one in the yard; that Indian or some of his companions had kept watch on the Macdonald yard, maybe for some time, but sure as hell since dusk last night up to sunrise this morning.

Colonel Donavon walked to a wagon tongue up off the ground, sat on it studying Gus Ruby. "I'd like you to pass a message to Mister Macdonald when he returns."

Gus nodded. "Be glad to."

Donavon arose and strolled toward his horse as he said, "The Bannocks got twenty-four hours to start back to their reservation." Donavon mounted before saying the rest of it. "I'll know if they're starting back. You can also tell Mister Macdonald a U.S. Marshal is at Fort Taylor. If the Bannocks aren't on the trail to their reservation within twenty-four hours, the Marshal will come out here, arrest Henry, Albert, and their paw and take them to a federal jail to be held for trial."

Gus eased down on the same wagon tongue as he said, "I'll pass it along, Colonel . . . By the way, Colonel, you ever been around Northern Cheyenne very much?"

Donavon did not reply. Colour showed in his face. He regarded the faded, un-shorn man with clear distaste. Gus said a little more, never once looking away from the officer nor hurrying his words.

"They're some of the best trackers an' scouts around. Any time there's fifteen in a bunch, you can bet your life they'll be bloody-hands . . . Tell you what, Colonel, when you get up a command to go after the Bannocks, look at your Cheyennes. If they got the mark of a red hand painted on their horses, they're going to kill. If you find any Bannocks, they'll kill them as sure as I'm settin' here, or maybe your soldiers if you try to stop them from doing it."

When Gus stopped speaking he drifted his gaze to the Indian on the horse with a spotted rump. The Indian looked back from an expressionless face with murder in his eyes.

Gus slowly smiled at the Indian before returning his attention to the officer to say a little more, and to say it slowly.

"I worked with the army up north. I know how the army looks at excuses,

Colonel. It *don't*. If there's a massacre of Bannocks by Northern Cheyenne, the same In'ians that helped wipe out Mister Custer's command . . . "

Gus paused smiling. He did not have to finish it, Colonel Donavon was regarding Gus as though he had just encountered the devil. His grip on the bridle reins was tight. "Just tell Mister Macdonald what I said," he snarled, swung half around and led off back the way he had come.

Gus built a smoke, leaned to watch the Colonel and his escort ride in the direction he had been told Fort Taylor had been established, ground the smoke under foot and arose, stretched mightily before sauntering out back to lean on the corral watching his horse.

Macdonald and his crew returned just short of evening. Alfred was with them. They had met him on the westerly range and clearly, from the expression on the faces of the father and son, they had discussed Gus Ruby's arrival at the rancheria, and what he had said then and later.

He nodded, the Macdonalds nodded back and were busy in the barn for fifteen minutes or so, then scattered. Henry, Will and Art Headley to wash up at the bunkhouse, Alfred and his father to stroll out back and join Gus at the corral.

Gus told them of the colonel's visit without explaining what he had said to Donavon. Alfred beat dust off his hat, looked at his father and said nothing. George Macdonald spat a couple of times before speaking.

"There's a hitch," he said quietly. "The Bannocks told Alfred they're through runnin' an' hidin'."

Gus nodded about that, the camp he had seen showed no signs of being struck, it had instead showed clear evidence the Bannocks were going to remain where they were. They had told Alfred they had done all the running they intended to do.

Now, Gus told the Macdonalds about his personal conversation with the colonel. George looked pleased but his oldest son looked slightly sceptical. Gus ignored that.

"It ain't my quarrel," he told George Macdonald, "but I guess when a man shoves his boots under another man's table he owes him something." Gus paused before continuing: "I loafed around this afternoon until you fellers got back; loafin' is a real good time for pondering. Mister Macdonald, that colonel left me feelin' like he's about ready to launch a campaign. Maybe he'll remember what I warned him about. Maybe he won't. I can tell you for a fact when he left the yard he was mad enough to chew bullets."

Alfred spoke for the first time. "The Bannocks won't move an' the colonel will . . . Paw . . . ?"

"I don't know, son. Right now I'm tired an' hungry."

Later, Henry met Gus down by the wagon shed. He knew about Donavon's visit and Gus's straight talk to the officer, but Henry was not especially glad. His own convictions had been firming up a long time. He told Gus that if there was a fight it wouldn't be just the Bannocks against the soldiers and the Cheyenne, it would be a fight between the Bannocks and as many reinforcements as the army would dispatch to help Donavon crush the Indians, then whip them all the way back to their reservation where they would be deprived of all firearms, all their horses, and their leaders would be imprisoned.

Gus studied the youngest boy before saying he was probably right, that the Bannocks refusing to run any more, plus the stubbornness of the Irish colonel, meant serious trouble for a fact, and when a man added in those Northern Cheyenne, there was a fine chance of a genuine massacre.

Henry scowled enquiringly at Gus. "Why would the army use Northern Cheyenne? Hell, only a short while back they was killin' soldiers as hard as they could. Them and the Sioux."

Gus was crafting a smoke and concentrated on getting it ready to fire up before he replied. "Henry, I expect that by the time you're my age you'll come to suspect that nothing's done by the army, by any part of the government, that don't smell of politics." Gus inhaled and exhaled before finishing what he had to say. "Politics, not In'ians nor the notion of fightin' them like Colonel Donavon aims to do, will ruin the career of an army officer. That was the notion I was tryin' to get across to Mister Donavon: turn Cheyenne and soldiers loose on those Bannocks, and it'll look like the Custer bleedin' ground all over again, an' Henry, nowadays newspapers get hold of something like that, make it ten times worse than it really was, an' Mister Donavon'll go back wherever he come from without his uniform."

Henry continued to frown. "Do you figure he'll really go after the Bannocks?"

Gus trickled smoke before answering.

"I wish I knew, Henry." Gus looked at the unhappy youth, slapped him lightly on the back and said, "For a feller just loafin' through, I sure rode right into a real one this time, didn't I?"

Henry raised his eyes to the lanky man's face. "That was clever, you tellin' the colonel in a nice way that — "

"He took it as a threat, Henry."

"Anyway, you put a bee in his hat. Maybe he'll let up on the Bannocks."

"He can't let up on 'em, Henry. They're off the reservation and refuse to go back. That's somethin' the army can't stand for, otherwise every blessed tomahawk will go back where he came from. Nope, Mister Donavon's got a ring-tailed roarer by the tail and dassn't hang on and dassn't let go. He's got to make a campaign or maybe just up an' resign his commission, an' from what I've seen of him he'd never in gawd's green world do that."

7

The First Casualty

ALFRED had failed to get the Bannock moving. His father did not like what that meant, so he decided to go talk to the headmen himself.

That was the day after he and both his sons, plus Will and Art had returned to the yard, after Macdonald had his discussion with Gus Ruby.

He told the others to make a sweep of the range over near Fort Taylor. When he got back he wanted to know if the colonel was getting ready to ride.

Macdonald did not include Gus in his decision for the other men. Gus was a guest.

They watched Macdonald ride away, this time going directly in the direction of the Bannock rancheria. Art Headley's squinted gaze followed his employer and wagged his head. Art had a premonition. He was not a superstitious man — any more than anyone else was — but from what he had heard lately, intuition, or something anyway, told him a showdown was imminent. He addressed Gus.

"What d'you think?"

Gus was candid as he watched the distant rider. "I think *if* he reaches the In'ian camp, unless he's a magician, he ain't goin' to do any better than Alfred did."

Macdonald's eldest son, standing close, put a hard look on Gus. "What d'you mean, *if* he reaches the camp?"

Gus continued to watch the distant rider and did not face around toward Alfred as he replied. "I been wastin' my breath; I'd bet a good horse the Cheyenne know about where that rancheria is, an' I'd bet another good horse they're up in those mountains somewhere." Gus finally faced around. "If the colonel has made his decision, he don't figure to fail. Most likely his job depends on not failing. If he's ready to start a campaign an' has his Cheyenne in the mountains watching," Gus made a small death's-head smile. "Your daddy more'n likely is goin' to ride right down someone's rifle barrel."

Not another word was said for a moment before Art Headley made a dry comment. "In that case maybe we'd best ride behind Mister Macdonald."

Gus considered the narrow-eyed older man. "Too late, partner. Them Cheyenne, if they're up there, will have rode during the night. By dawn they'll have both the trail to the camp an' the camp itself under observation." For a moment Gus hung fire. To him this was like explaining something to children; it was both frustrating and tiresome. He had made himself clear several times. Those confounded Idahoans were as thick as oak.

Art and perhaps Will Stratton seemed to understand, at least they were silent.

115

But Alfred was made of different metal. He started to berate Gus, who took the abuse looking relaxed. Right up until Henry lit into his brother. Alfred turned and struck without warning. The blow was not especially damaging, but it was as much a surprise to Henry, who had never been struck by his brother before, as it was to Headley and Stratton.

Gus moved in, spun Alfred by the shoulder and struck an upward blow which travelled no farther than his belt buckle, but which evidently had the power of a mule kick.

Alfred went down and rolled over, face down. Headley and Stratton gazed from the unconscious man on the ground to Gus Ruby, who had already drawn his sixgun. Whatever the pair of hired riders might have done, it was now too late for physical action, but not for words. Will sounded almost chagrined when he said, "You didn't have to hit him. He's got a right to his opinion."

Gus let go a ragged breath. "Mister,

if it had been just the cussin' out, I wouldn't have hit him, but the damned idiot still don't understand. His paw is very likely on his last ride."

Henry gazed at the unconscious man, slowly raised his eyes to Gus Ruby and said. "I'll go with you."

Henry was Gus's favourite of the entire Macdonald clan. He smiled at the youth. "You really want to help — keep your brother here even if you have to tie him to a post." Before walking toward the barn for his horse Gus spoke to the hired riders. "You gents do as the boss said — go scout up the soldiers. Be sure that's all you do." He stopped in the front barn opening. "One thing I ought to tell you: I been stalked an' ambushed and chased . . . I can see skulkers shaggin' me without even turnin' to look." He smiled. "Watch them soldiers. I'll be back when you see me coming."

They watched the second horseman leave the yard, but this time riding due south in a slow lope, the kind of gait that covered miles without tiring the horse. They watched Gus parallel the mountains until he was out of sight.

Art looked at Will and Henry. He seemed to be waiting for someone to speak. When no one did he jutted his chin downward. "We better tie Alfred. If we don't, when he comes around he'll give us all we can handle . . . Henry?"

The youth headed for the barn for two pigging strings, one for his brother's wrists, one for his ankles.

The sun was climbing, birds in the grass which still had dew on it were happily hunting insects between moments of the kind of bird-song that reflected a pure delight in being alive.

The air was glass-clear, so clear Gus could see huge trees by sky-lining them which were at least five miles distant.

Summer was pleasant. In Idaho summers usually remained pleasant longer than other, particularly lowland, areas of the west.

The sorrel seemed to have recovered

118

fully from his day-long ride yesterday. He kept at the rocking-chair lope until, when Gus looked back he could see nothing of the yard or its buildings.

Gus had made some mental estimates as he rode. When he eventually let the horse change course a little at a time until they were parallelling huge trees, row after row of them stair-stepping their way up rough mountainsides, to anyone watching he would be backgrounded by the shadows of primeval timberland, and slackened the pace because from here on he had no illusions. To reach the Bannock rancheria he and the sorrel were going to have to do some climbing and some descending. His goal was somewhere behind the rancheria, southward.

There would be Bannock, and more than likely Cheyenne, on points of vantage where they could see every yard of the trails Gus had used yesterday, the same route George Macdonald would be following today.

He had to take his chances on other Bannocks watching the southward country, but if they were, they would not be doing it as closely and intently as they would be watching the opposite direction.

He was right about one thing; those wash-outs between canyons were very rare, which meant he had to use game trails to reach topouts, and more game trails to descend.

He did not believe he would arrive in the area of the rancheria in time to prevent whatever might happen to Macdonald; he was reasonably confident that, as *coyote* as the Cheyenne would be, now that the Bannock knew they had enemies close to their camp, they would have more than the usual number of spies in high places. These would recognise Macdonald. They would also recognise anyone else, especially alien Indians.

It was a gamble. The Cheyenne might shoot Macdonald. Gus doubted that the colonel would have authorised anything like that, but he also knew the Cheyenne.

He also reasoned that one gun shot in those canyons would be heard by every Bannock who was not deaf, which would probably mean the shooter would never live to reach open country again, which was slight satisfaction, particularly if the Cheyenne killed Macdonald.

The sorrel horse did not hesitate. Like any good horse he did what was required of him, leaving such things as founder, crippling, or broken-wind to the man whom he trusted on his back.

Gus Ruby was fond of the sorrel. It may have been as 'knowledgeable authorities' claimed, single rangemen found a substitute for a family, or a wife, in their horses, which was the typical hogwash 'knowledgeable authorities' dealt in. Rangemen took good care of an honest horse. Usually before seeing to their own comfort. A good using horse was not a substitute for anything, he was a professional horseman's friend and partner.

Gus made it as easy as he could on the sorrel. When he 'blew' him he never did it atop a rim where cold air was, he rested the sorrel where there was no cold wind.

It caused delay, but that couldn't be helped if a man had a conscience and a 'feeling' for animals, which Gus had in good measure.

But by the time they reached a grassy ledge behind the rancheria and could look down on it from the camouflaging shadows of huge old fir trees, the sun had moved well away from its meridian. As Gus stood beside the sorrel he was half of the opinion that whatever Macdonald had ridden into, had already happened, but he had not heard a gunshot, which in this kind of country would reverberate for a great distance.

He had no illusion about being alone and, as he was tightening the cinch to mount, three wraiths appeared among the trees. Hoping at least one of them understood English, he called out. "Howdy. I'm the feller who was in your camp yesterday."

Evidently none of the Indians understood, but knowing they had been seen, they stepped clear of their trees and stood, Winchesters in both hands.

Gus tried something else. "*How cola*," he called in Dahkota. "*Wasicun . . .* " He couldn't remember the word for 'friendly' but it did not matter, the Indians stood like statues.

Gus tied the sorrel and approached the nearest Indian, who was a short, bull-built individual with weathered skin and a low forehead. When he was close enough to be recognised the Bannock said something in his own language. His companions loosened a little but not entirely.

Gus asked if any of them understood English. His answer was a blank look so he threw up his hands, went to mount the sorrel and start down toward the rancheria.

The Indians followed on foot, leaving other Bannocks who had remained in hiding, behind.

The distance was not great. He and his companions were seen while still on the down-slope. An alarm was sounded which sounded like someone moving his tongue swiftly as he called out.

This call was picked up until Indians were facing the sidehill in considerable numbers. Only when Gus reached flat ground and was closer, did one Indian yell to the others that the whiteman was the same one who had been at their camp the day before. To Gus's surprise the ugly heavy-set dark woman whose stew he had eaten, pushed past, stopped and smiled. She said something indistinguishable and laughed.

Gus dismounted near that brush shelter where he and Alfred Macdonald had talked the day before. One of the same older bucks emerged, considered Gus for a long time showing no expression, then called to someone. Another Indian, much younger turned back through the crowd.

The headman gestured for Gus to enter the shelter. He smiled while shaking his head. While this was occurring a large Indian Gus had never seen before came up and said, "Welcome," and offered a thick hand, whiteman-fashion. Gus shook and asked if George Macdonald was in the camp.

The big Indian's manner was solemn. He gave a delayed answer. "He is here," and pointed to the brush shelter. "Hurt."

Gus loosened the cinch of his horse, handed its reins to the big buck and went in the direction of the brush shelter the Indian had indicated.

The big Indian passed Gus's reins to a youth with instructions for its care then also crossed to the brush shelter, which he entered but had to duck his head to clear the baulk.

There was an impassive Bannock woman on her knees beside a buffalo hide pallet. George Macdonald was lying on it.

He recognised Gus and croaked a question. "You sure have a knack for turning up, don't you?"

Gus smiled, said nothing and, with his eyes finally accustomed to the gloom, crossed over and hunkered beside the pallet. The woman looked her disapproval but said nothing.

Back by the doorway the big Indian stood as though to block the opening if he had to. He was unarmed and bare from the waist up where his hide showed skin under which muscle was tightly packed.

Gus said, "They got you, eh?"

Macdonald accepted water from the poker-faced woman before answering. "They got me. I had to take a chance they would watch but not shoot. Otherwise I couldn't have got up here as soon as I did."

"Did you see the one that shot you?"

"No, but it don't matter, I got here and palavered."

Gus let his breath out slowly, there

was sticky blood on the cowman's shirt. Macdonald saw Gus's look and spoke while breathing shallowly. "Hit me in the side. He must have been trying for a heart-shot but was maybe a little too far to one side. It busted three ribs and made a gouge. This woman's patched it up good." Macdonald reached over and patted the impassive woman's hand. Her eyes smiled but her face didn't.

Macdonald asked what Gus was doing here. The answer was simple, he was at the rancheria because he had followed Macdonald, and the reason he had followed him was because he knew as surely as he knew his name Colonel Donavon's Cheyenne would be scouting up the countryside around the rancheria.

"Figured if I could get up here, and be behind them, I might be able to lend a hand."

"Where is Alfred?"

The question took Gus by surprise. "Back at the yard. Henry and the other two went to scout around that fort. Alfred's . . . minding the home place."

George Macdonald, who hated liars, was experienced at recognising both a lie and the expression of lying. He began to scowl. "Alfred wouldn't stay back. Henry might but Alfred wouldn't."

Gus settled on the ground. "Alfred and I had an argument. I left him lying near the tie-rack . . . Now wait a minute, he'll be all right, maybe have a sore jaw for a while but — "

"Argument about what?"

"Nothing, really. He cussed me out and I hit him. When you get back he'll tell you about it." Gus pushed up to his feet and was about to turn away when the wounded cowman spoke. "That big bronco back at the opening. Him an' another buck was real close lying still in rocks. They didn't see the feller with the rifle until he raised up, to look down at the rancheria, which was understandable but it was a mistake. They clubbed him senseless, tied him and brought him down here."

Gus said, "Dead?"

"No, but he's got one helluva a headache." Macdonald said something guttural to the large man by the opening, then addressed Gus. "He'll take you where they got him."

Gus followed the big Indian. For the first time he noticed there were more women and pups in the encampment than men.

That more than likely was a good thing. If it meant nothing else it indicated that the Bannocks had taken the warnings seriously which had been passed to them.

8

The Main Problem

WHEN Gus ducked into the gloomy brush shelter where a muscled up Bannock was sitting as expressionless as a stone and another one was sitting just beyond the entrance, he recognised the injured Cheyenne even before his eyes became completely adjusted to the gloom.

It was the rider of the spotted-rump horse who had accompanied Colonel Donavon into the Macdonald yard when Gus was the only one around.

The same Indian whose sardonic faint smile Gus remembered. The Cheyenne recognised Gus but indicated recognition by only a flicker of his eyes.

Gus sat down, rolled and lighted a smoke. The strong-looking Cheyenne never once took his gaze off Gus. He did show that expression of cold superiority he had shown at their previous meeting.

Gus trickled smoke, gave stare for stare with his adversary while the Bannock who had been guarding the prisoner watched both men. Besides an old cap and ball pistol in his belt, this Bannock had a twelve-inch-long Meshing knife in a beaded scabbard — on the same belt.

Gus spoke quietly in English. "What's your name?"

The Cheyenne may have been a prisoner with both wrists tied by a rawhide thong but he was not afraid. "Many Horses. What's yours!"

Gus tipped ash. This time he was not addressing someone who looked blank at everything he said. "What were you doing when the Bannock caught you?"

"Scouting for Colonel Donavon."

"Alone?"

The Indian neither blinked nor

shifted his eyes, but neither did he reply.

"Fifteen Northern Cheyenne," Gus said, leaning to punch out his quirley, "amounts to a war party . . . Why? You're many miles from Cheyenne country . . . Why?"

"You know why. Scout for the army."

"Fifteen Cheyenne?"

"This is a big country. We never been over here before. We had to cross Crow and Shoshoni territory, enemies of my people."

"How many Cheyenne are in these mountains?" Gus expected no reply but he got one, and it shocked him.

Many Horses's black eyes bored into Gus when he replied. "Many soldiers come. Cheyenne know where this place is. Many soldiers will be showed this place."

"When?" Gus asked, and this time he got no answer, but the Indian stared steadily at him. Many Horses had meant exactly what he had said.

132

Gus wondered what the Macdonald riders would see. If they saw the soldiers readying for a campaign they would tell what they saw when he got back. But — if the colonel acted on the advice of his Cheyenne, and perhaps even if he didn't, he would screen his preparations.

Gus had to assume the campaign would begin soon. He and Many Horses looked steadily at one another. The Bannock sitting in shadows stirred, which broke the mood. Gus arose and walked back out into the sunshine. The Bannock were finally acting subdued, probably fearful. They had visual evidence that the Cheyenne were in their territory, and while Bannocks were courageous warriors, they were not and never had been in the class of the Northern Cheyenne.

Gus returned to Macdonald's gloomy shelter. A different squaw was with the wounded man. She was younger, more attractive, and not quite as inhibited. When Gus grunted down into a

133

sitting position the woman said in clear English, "He is sleeping."

Gus considered her from an expressionless face. There had been no accent, no short sentences, no hesitation when she spoke.

She returned his look. "I am Southern Shoshoni. I was the teacher at the school on the Bannock reservation."

"You broke out with them?"

The woman's eyes flashed. "It makes no difference who people are, they don't deserve to starve to death. Yes, I broke out with them. And you?"

Gus admired the woman's obvious indignation. "I was just passing through."

"Why did you stop?"

Gus rubbed a stubbly jaw. She had asked a good question. Before he could think of an answer she said, "Because you don't think people should be deliberately starved to death?"

Gus stopped stroking his chin. That hadn't been his reason at all, but he *had* allowed himself to get involved, so he shrugged. "Maybe something like that. Right now I got to figure a way to get Mister Macdonald back to his yard."

She considered Gus solemnly before she spoke. "You can't move him. He is no longer bleeding. If you move him and go very far, he will start bleeding. It will kill him."

Gus considered the grey, beard-stubbled face of the sleeping man. Maybe it would be all right to leave him at the rancheria. For a fact the Bannock had done very well by him. But there was another consideration. If what Many Horses had said was true, if the rancheria was attacked soon, perhaps within the next few days. Macdonald on his back and helpless could very easily become a fatality along with many Bannock.

He gazed at the Shoshoni woman. "It's a damned mess," he said, and for the first time her liquid dark eyes showed something besides indignation.

"It's not the fault of the Indians . . . What is your name?"

"Gus. Gus Ruby."

"It's not the fault of the Indians, Mister Ruby. Invaders in their country have turned everything topsy-turvy. Cheyenne should not help white men destroy Bannock. Only a short time ago Cheyenne and Sioux were killing soldiers and settlers. Now, Cheyenne are helping the white men destroy Bannock. Do you know what it was like for the Bannock on that reservation?"

Gus only knew what he had heard. He did not answer, he gazed at the sleeping cowman.

The woman said, "The Cheyenne and Sioux will be on a reservation as soon as the white man no longer needs them to help him against other Indians." She paused to also look at George Macdonald, whose slumber did not allow him to hear this discussion, which he surely would have enjoyed.

"Mister Ruby, it is the white man who takes ten steps forward and six steps back. It is the white man who steals everything even the life and soul from the Indian."

Gus raised a hand to stop the angry flow of words. "Lady, we're not going to settle right from wrong today. My concern is for Mister Macdonald. And for the way those In'ians outside are bein' ganged up on."

"Do you have a solution for the Bannock, Mister Ruby?"

"Nope, I sure don't, except the one Mister Macdonald and his son tried to get them to do. Go back on the reservation."

She stared at him. For a little while she had thought he might be different. She had been sitting on her haunches. Now, she arose looking down at the sleeping man before she walked out of the hutment leaving Gus sitting there with his quandary.

Two older Bannock came into the gloomy house. One nodded to Gus and they both leaned to look closely at the sleeping man, then, without a word they both departed.

Gus went after them. The language

difficulty was resolved by the Shoshoni woman. She offered to interpret. As she made the offer her expression was blank and her gaze at Gus was as detached and indifferent as she could make it.

He asked her to have the older men tell her what their plans were. When the answer came back there was a glint of cold satisfaction in the woman's eyes. "They will have the women and children taken to a safe canyon and put guards on the high places around them. And the men, old and young, will make ambushes among the passes leading to this place. They will fight, Mister Ruby, the same as you would do if you were an Indian."

As he listened and watched something in the back of his head told him he should find out more about this woman who spoke better English than he did.

When he made no immediate comment she asked if he was satisfied. He wasn't satisfied, he had worked for the army, knew its strength and resolve, but he nodded to her and walked away.

This was hopeless.

He went to find his sorrel horse. Black eyes watched his every move but no one spoke nor appeared to be watching when he looked around.

On his way out of the canyon he ignored the strong possibility that both Bannock and Cheyenne were watching him. What he had to tell Henry and Alfred was that without a miracle their father would probably be killed.

What the two hired riders and Henry had to tell him when he eventually got back to the yard did not make him feel any better.

The two rangemen had seen soldiers preparing to take the field. There were two Cheyenne with them. It required little imagination to guess where the other thirteen Cheyenne were.

Alfred would not talk to Gus, which annoyed him a little, but with more important things on his mind, such as the way Henry and the pair of hired riders appeared to look to Gus for leadership, he decided from being a somewhat indifferent partisan to one who was now fully involved, he had to search for solutions.

And right at the moment he found none. If the situation for the Bannock and George Macdonald was not hopeless he could think of nothing that was more hopeless.

He asked the three men watching him un-saddle if there were neighbours they could count on. Art and Will shook their heads. Alfred, sounding vindictive, said even if there were, the closest source of possible help was over in Clarksville, which was a round trip ride of twelve miles, providing the townsmen were ready to ride when someone got over there, which of course they could not be expected to be.

Gus smiled wanly at Alfred. "Got a better suggestion?" he asked, and before the eldest son could reply, the youngest one said, "The reservation."

Alfred scoffed. "The reservation is thirty miles from here."

Henry nodded, conceding it hadn't been a wise suggestion.

Art Headley, the rangeman with perpetually squinted eyes had an idea. He prefaced the idea with a brief explanation of why he had thought of it. "Some years back I was in southern Oregon. At least that's where I thought I was until I seen soldiers ridin' along; dark men with red do-dads on their hats . . . They was Messicans. I was in the north part of California. They was ridin' in a hurry to catch some 'Mericans with a soldier-escort against the northerly mountains . . . Later, I heard how that scuffle come out. I don't know that it'll work here — but them 'Mericans seen dust from couple hundred horses racin' to catch them. The 'Mericans didn't number half, maybe a third, that many, so they run back the way they'd come into the mountains an' left behind a little brass cannon and most of their gatherings."

No one spoke for a moment, each man waited for the rest of the story. Art gave it dryly. "Them Messicans, maybe fifty, sixty of 'em, pulled up big bushes, let them hang back two to a rider. The dust looked like a whole blessed army."

The silence lingered until Alfred scornfully said, "That don't make sense. Why didn't the Americans see what was causing the dust?"

Headley looked straight at Alfred when he replied. "They made their charge a little before sunrise, when there was daylight but not very good visibility."

Again the silence closed down. Gus thought of variations of the idea and suddenly said, "Hell! We could round up a bunch of cattle and do that . . . Wait until evening." He looked at Art Headley. "How long would you figure it'll take the soldiers to reach the passes?"

Headley's partner, Will Stratton

replied. "The way they was goin' about it, my guess is that they won't leave the fort before morning. Early; maybe a tad before sunrise."

Alfred suddenly came alive. "We got the rest of the day to make a gather. If anyone sees what's goin' on — what the hell — it's close to roundup time. Hold the herd until someone scouts close an' can hear the army on the move. Stampede the cattle right into them. Scatter soldiers to hell and back, bust up their pack train. An' we could be gone before they knew what happened."

Again silence descended. Alfred's plan was a variation of Art's suggestion. In fact it sounded more likely to achieve success than Art's idea. Henry nodded at his brother. They hadn't spoken since Gus had knocked Alfred unconscious.

Gus looked from face to face. Each one showed a glimmer of approval. He said, "Henry . . . ?" The youngest son nodded. "If we get to making the gather right now. It'll take all the daylight we got left to gather that many cattle."

Henry was correct, there was not a whole lot of daylight left. They hurriedly went to saddle fresh animals. Henry was also right about making the gather. With little reason to gang together even though by nature cattle were herd animals, they had to ride hard over many miles to bring their herd together. They barely beat dusk.

Nervous cattle make noise. That troubled Gus a little even though Fort Taylor was a fair distance from the gather and its drovers. He was not sure Colonel Donavon wouldn't have spies watching the Macdonald place. The colonel had reason to consider the Macdonalds as antagonists.

Gus had to hope, if there was someone from the fort watching, he might assume the roundup was a reasonable part of ranching, even though Gus or the riders with him, would not have viewed a wild round up so late in the day to be a commonplace event, but rather extraordinary.

He and Alfred decided they would nighthawk, which left the others to go back to the ranch, get some sleep and return after a few hours with food and cold coffee.

Alfred had acted differently since his variation of Art Headley's suggestion had been agreed upon. As he and Gus hunkered in the cooling night, their horses hobbled, the saddles removed and the saddle blankets around their shoulders, Henry asked for details of his father's injuries. Gus gave them and watched the younger man look out where cattle were bedding down.

Gus added a little more. "There's a Shoshoni school marm doctorin' him. She's doin' a good job. Barrin' the wound gettin' infected — an' figurin' the Cheyenne don't try to shoot everythin' with two legs they can find, I'd guess he's got a good chance."

Alfred said, "Damned Cheyenne. Why are they buyin' into somethin' so far from their range?"

Gus made a guess. "After Custer an' the way the army run them down afterwards and killed what they could find, I'd say they're toadyin' to get back into favour."

Before George Macdonald's oldest son could pursue this subject, Gus also said, "If your idea works, we scatter the army an' its pack train, maybe we can rescue your paw, but that'll only be the beginning. You understand that?"

Alfred tucked the saddle blanket closer before answering. "I reckon. The army'll be after the Macdonalds — and you."

Gus had thought of that earlier and had dismissed the idea. "My guess is that they'll have their hands full with the stampede. Even if it's close to daylight, they're not likely to see riders in the dust. What I meant was, when the colonel gets routed, he's goin' to be mad as hell. He'll send for reinforcements, lick his wounds until they arrive, then he'll come into

146

your yard and take the bunch of us into military custody, which he'll have a right to do. Alfred, after he does that, an' has a bigger command, those Bannocks will be finished, no matter how wide or deep they go into the mountains. The army don't call off an In'ian hunt just because of mountains."

Alfred sat huddled in his blanket. In watery poor starlight it struck Gus that Alfred's Indian side was particularly prominent. Gus went to work rolling a smoke for supper, the cattle were settled, neither he nor Alfred would have to ride nighthawk. It wasn't as though this was a genuine roundup when cattle would attempt to leave the herd. If that happened tonight, as it almost invariably did with a gather, there would still be more than enough cattle left.

Alfred roused out of his reverie, looked at the star-shot vault of heaven and said, "Do you think my brother has been right all along, that directly now there won't be a place for Indians?"

147

Gus had considered this a few times, off and on, but had never truly thought about it. "Well, Alfred, they are going to be here, aren't they? The army or anyone else can't make them disappear."

"But what will become of them?"

Gus had no answer. Like most men of his time he had thought only in terms of fighting Indians, scattering them, keeping them away from even the environs of the white man's world.

He smoked, pondered, and decided that the way for most conquered people was to blend with their conquerors. Maybe not all at once, but over generations. Otherwise — sure as hell they would cease to exist.

"I expect as the number of whites increases an' the land, the game animals an' the unsettled country decreases, both sides'll have to figure things out, come to an understanding."

Alfred's reply to that used bitter words, but his tone of voice was surprisingly free of bitterness. "Maybe.

Sure as hell fighting hasn't accomplished much for In'ians. But I'd guess if gettin' along happens it'll not be for a long time. Not in your or my lifetime."

Gus killed his smoke and changed the subject. It was past midnight, the night was turning cold, the cattle were quiet, the heavens were a blaze with an infinity of tiny bright lights.

"Alfred, you'n your brother stay well back. If soldiers see me, or Stratton or Headley it won't matter because we'll be gone before they can do much, but the Macdonalds, man and boy, got roots here. Pass that along when you see Henry."

"We're not speaking," Alfred stated.

"Don't be a damn fool. There's no law says you two got to agree on everything, but he's blood kin. That counts over everything else."

When Alfred might have spoken, he instead held up a hand for almost half a minute before he said, "You hear anything?"

Gus hadn't but evidently some of the

cattle had, they had come up out of their beds peering northeasterly.

Gus arose. So much for breakfast. He went to rig out his horse as did Alfred. By the time they were finished, standing beside their animals listening, Henry had arrived.

He dismounted and passed around food bundles wrapped with cloth. He too listened, because the sound was greater now, he barely more than spoke to Gus and his brother before the three of them swung astride.

They sat like wraiths listening, watching more cattle leave their beds. Eventually, when the sound of mounted men and pack animals could be distinctly identified, all the cattle were up, the horses of the waiting men were standing heads-up, little ears pointing in the same direction.

Gus said, "Fan out. Don't let them see you."

9

An Unexpected Disaster

WHEN running cattle were audible to the troopers, the packers and their animals, the sound seemed to be coming from all directions. Darkness heightened the fear of animals and some men.

When the cattle reached the column and could be recognised for what they were, rank after rank of terrified large animals running without heed for what was ahead, men fired guns, yelled, swung their animals to escape in wild dashes, Henry and Alfred reined back, gauged events by sound, then turned back the way they had come riding without haste.

Behind them the furor, black dust in a black night and gunfire mixed with shouts, indicated that the stampede had accomplished its purpose. The others had been in the yard a short while before Gus arrived. He was satisfied, but only for what he considered the initial phase. As he swung off he told the Macdonalds to saddle fresh animals, that with the army in temporary disarray, they now had the hardest objective to achieve.

"Sneak through the Cheyenne around the Bannock rancheria, get your paw out of there, an' maybe find the Cheyenne an' run them off too."

Alfred and Henry went after fresh horses without a word until they were behind the barn, then Alfred smiled bleakly at his brother as he said, "That feller must've been a general, or something."

The three of them left Headley and Stratton at the yard standing in darkness. There were no sounds of difficulty north and easterly, but the colonel would recognise by now that the destruction of his orderly, premeditated assault, had been scattered not by accident, since even greenhorns knew cattle did not stampede right over the top of a soldier column without being positioned to do that, especially at night.

If they could have seen and heard the colonel as predawn light firmed up, they would have been awed. Once his scattered force had reassembled at Fort Taylor, with stragglers coming in most of the early morning, singly and in little groups, the officer swore and gesticulated, stamped and made threats until a junior officer with less temper suggested that a muster be held, to which the colonel agreed, then stamped into his small office, slammed the door after himself and went directly to the little cupboard where his cigars and whiskey were kept. He drank deeply of one and furiously fired up the other. Never, in a long stint in the army, had he been so furious, and as sure as night followed day those had been Macdonald cattle, and the Macdonalds had been behind that stampede.

He flung down at his desk, wrote furiously then went bellowing for his orderly with orders to ride to the nearest telegraph office and send that message to the general commanding his district.

He was in his office again after breakfast when that red-faced old campaigner, the ranking non-commissioned officer, arrived to report.

They had lost two men unaccounted for, three mules with full packs and had six lame horses. The old campaigner stood at indifferent, almost slouching attention and waited.

Donavon sat a moment with both arms on his desk, then shot up to his feet and swore a blue streak, things which did not interest the sergeant very much, he had seen officers explode many times, and he knew something they did not know; furious commanders were likely to shout bad orders. The old campaigner waited.

Donavon turned on him with a thick vein throbbing at the temple.

"It was those gawdamned Macdonalds. Sergeant, take as many men as you want, go back out there and bring all three of them — and that other feller, whatever his name is — back here. Lock 'em in the brig and throw the key away!"

The sergeant shifted stance, waited until Donavon was back at his desk, then spoke. "Sir, I didn't see no riders, did you? None of the other fellers saw any riders."

Donavon rocked back spearing the older man with angry eyes. He did not answer the question. "Those damned cattle didn't charge into the column on their own. You know as well as I — "

"Sir. Maybe they did. I know just this much about cattle, when they are scairt in the dark — they run without no direction or reason."

"Sergeant, gawdammit, that was deliberate!"

"Colonel, that spokesman for the Cheyenne said they shot the old man an' the Bannocks got him at their camp."

"Well; he has two sons hasn't he? They're like the old man. And that feller who sassed me in the yard. How about him?"

The sergeant sighed under his breath. "All right, Sir, I'll take a party, bring them back and lock 'em up. But — "

"*Sergeant!*"

The old campaigner returned to the yard where daylight was breaking, stood a moment in the chill then went in the direction of the horse area. There was one man down there, the others were at mess. The sergeant sat on a small keg as the enlisted man on horse-detail sauntered up, leaned on his manure fork and said, "Well, we got six lame horses, Sergeant."

The older man nodded, looked at the much younger man with a wag of his head. "You got an occupation?" he asked.

"Soldiering."

"You know anything else; you got a

trade by any chance?"

The enlisted man shrugged. "Back east I was a hames maker."

"Was you good at it?" the older man asked, deadly serious.

"Yes, I was good at it."

"When your enlistment is up, boy, go back to it," the old campaigner said, and stood up. "Whatever else you do, boy, don't re-enlist . . . I'll need six horses rigged for riding. I'll be back in about a half hour."

The enlisted man continued to lean on his fork until the sergeant was out of sight, then he went back to work. He had no intention of re-enlisting. He'd only joined the army to get as far as he could from a woman who had made his life miserable and who, hopefully, had either forgotten him by now or would have by the time his hitch was up next year.

The sergeant caught them as they emerged from the mess hall. He called each man by name, told him to stand aside, waited until all the others had passed, then told them where the colonel wanted them to go, and why.

No one spoke. They were tired men, rumpled, un-shaven, not in a good mood despite just having taken the pleats out of their bellies. One of them a short, thick man whose head and neck were the same size and whose pale eyes bored into the sergeant, sullenly said, "Sarge, just answer one question for me."

The old campaigner eyed the pale-eyed man impassively. He and the bull-necked man knew each other very well. Except for being an unpredictable periodic drunk, the pale-eyed man would have also been a sergeant. In fact he had made that rank three times over the past nine years and would likely make it again before his re-enlistment ran out.

"Why don't the colonel just set here until we get reinforcements? This ain't goin' to be one of the usual 'show the flag' affairs, not after what happened last night. They're organised, an' they're resourceful."

The old campaigner regarded the other man without blinking. "That's good thinking, Otto . . . Why don't you go talk to the colonel about what he ought to do?" The sergeant jerked his head and started in the direction of the horse area. Behind them the pale-eyed man brought up the rear without so much as glancing at the command hut as he and his comrades walked past.

Newday warmth arrived, which was a blessing in one way and was not a blessing in another way. The party with the old campaigner in charge rode in the direction of the Macdonald place with warmth on them — and dozed most of the way. Full guts with pleasant heat on tired bodies achieved that inevitable result.

The sergeant noticed, understood and made no objection until they had the buildings in sight. What caused him to delay grumbling his companions to alertness was a very large thin and wavery cloud of dust in the middle distance.

The detail halted to consider this; one man — there was always one — came up with a shoot-from-the-hip notion. He said. "It's them damned cattle goin' back where they come from."

A couple of men looked at him, said nothing and returned their attention to the dust. Cattle did not go all together anywhere, even if they were on the move to water or shade or better feed; they straggled along, sometimes a mile or more separating the leaders from the drag. All soldiers or anyone else had to know was that driven cattle made dust, straggling did not.

The pale-eyed, bull-necked man squared up in the saddle with a suggestion for the sergeant. "A couple of us could go over there and see what's going on."

The old campaigner turned slowly. "Otto, we *know* what's goin' on. Cattle is on the move." He straightened up and started ahead toward the yard and buildings. The others followed.

The sergeant rode the last hundred and fifty yards frowning. The yard was empty, no horses nickered at the arrival of other horses, the house looked as empty as did the yard.

Where the sergeant drew rein in the centre of the yard he had that feeling of emptiness he had felt before in abandoned places.

He swung off, looped his reins at the tie-rack and started toward the main-house, tucking gauntlets under and over his belt as he walked along.

On the porch he rattled the door, waited and rattled it again. He was turning away when a shadow moved at the westerly end of the long porch. An Indian said, "There ain't nobody here. We looked."

The sergeant studied the Indian. He was not the leader of the Cheyenne but he was one of the same party. Before the sergeant could speak the Indian strode closer, eyed the waiting men over by the barn, hung his Winchester in the crook of one arm and gestured with the other arm.

"They got Many Horses," he said.

The sergeant scowled. "Who's got Many Horses?"

"Bannocks. They got him an' the old man who lives here. He's hurt. They got him in one of their — "

"Where are the other two that live here — and that other feller who runs with them?"

The Indian did not know. He had come out of the mountains to scout up what that gunfire had been about last night.

The sergeant leaned on a porch upright regarding the Cheyenne. "Where are the other Cheyenne?"

"In the mountains. Got around the Bannock camp. They're waitin' for the army."

The sergeant blew out a hard breath. "Well, the army got run over last night by a bunch of cattle. We went back to the fort."

The Indian did not look pleased. "The army," he said gruffly, "was supposed to come into the mountains this morning. We was told that and we been waiting."

"Well, my friend, the army ain't comin' this morning an' maybe not tomorrow morning."

"When?" the Indian asked.

The sergeant had no ready answer. "I don't know. The colonel didn't tell me. Maybe in a couple of days." The sergeant had no difficulty interpreting the look on the face of the Indian. "When I get back I'll tell him the Cheyenne are in place around the Bannock. I'll say you fellers want to get this thing over with. I'll tell him you're waiting for the army to go up there."

The Indian's expression was unpleasant. His father had raided with The Bull and Crazy Horse. He had told his son the soldiers could not be relied upon. Clearly this was in the Indian's mind now as he stared sourly at the sergeant.

He turned on his heel, disappeared around the corner of the house. The sergeant trudged back to his waiting escort, looked up and said, "They expected us. We didn't show up. I told him I had no idea when we would arrive. He turned and walked away." The sergeant puckered his eyes swung into the saddle and turned back. As they were leaving the Macdonald yard he said the rest of it. "Anybody in a bettin' mood? I'll lay five to one them In'ians will pull out. Maybe even bypass the post and keep on ridin' until they're back in their own country."

No one took him up on the offer. They'd had a long ride for nothing. There was very little conversation on the return trip. Even when they reached the grinder and were dismissed, they led their animals down to be cared for and still spoke very little to one another.

The colonel listened to the sergeant while leaning on his desk chewing an un-lighted cigar. When the sergeant finished, the officer carefully put his cigar aside, leaned back and said, "I wanted the Macdonalds. I should have told you to keep on riding until you found them."

The sergeant let that go past because it didn't make a lick of sense. He had no idea where to search, unless it was some of those canyons, which by now would be full of bushwhacking Bannocks.

The officer asked if the sergeant had told the Cheyenne to come in. The sergeant hadn't because that had not been part of his orders. He shook his head. "Everythin' that In'ian said to me, an' everythin' I said to him I already told you. I didn't know you wanted 'em back at the fort."

The colonel said, "Get some rest. You've earned it."

Out front in late-day sunlight the old campaigner rolled his eyes. He was not angry or frustrated, he had been a soldier too long to have those feelings, but his disgust was deep and abiding, something he had felt often over the years.

The sergeant sought his hutment, flung off everything but his underwear and went to bed. He did not awaken until the bugler played The Colours, meaning another day had ended. He got dressed, went over to the sluice to shave and wash, returned with limp towel over one shoulder, ferreted for his box of not-quite-smoked-down cigars, selected the longest one, which had splayed at one end, lighted up and went outside to sit in the cooling late day with evening on the way.

He had not mentioned his wager that no one had taken him up on, nor the dust from a bunch of cattle they had all seen and had speculated about. One, in the sergeant's view would be about as important to the colonel as the other.

He had been right about most things, so maybe he was entitled not to be right about them all.

The red-maned lieutenant, junior in rank to a captain and the colonel, and also junior in years to most of the enlisted men, and all of the officers as well as being junior to the old campaigner, arrived to share the sergeant's bench before Taps. He was interested in the lack of success of the sergeant's detail. Not uncommonly officers did not commiserate with failures by enlisted men. Also not uncommonly they revelled in that kind of failure. As the sergeant related what had occurred, the youthful junior officer said, "But didn't you realise under the circumstances the colonel would have wanted the Cheyenne to come in?"

The old campaigner finished his cigar, ground it underfoot and without another word turned to enter his hutment and light the lamp.

The lieutenant wandered in the general direction of his own hutment, encountered the colonel and said that after listening to the sergeant, he could understand the colonel being angry, the sergeant should have known the colonel would want the Cheyenne to return to the fort.

Donavon, although an officer himself, had not achieved that rank through a military education. He looked for a long moment at the lieutenant then said. "Mister, I foresee a long and excellent career for you in the army," nodded and walked away.

The lieutenant was so elated he rushed to his hutment to write his parents about the colonel's praise.

The colonel, on the other hand, walked slowly to his own lodging, sank down in a chair and rolled his eyes as he reached for the lamp to light it. Anyone who could unintentionally polish the colonel's apple in as godforsaken place as Fort Taylor located at the farthest reach of nowhere, should advance rapidly once he had served his 'field time' and would be re-assigned to some area headquarters where a general commanded.

10

Another Long Day

GUS knew if he and the Macdonalds entered the mountainous country, no matter how clever they tried to be, or how careful and wary, they would be seen, if for no other reason than because the Cheyenne, and now the Bannock as well, had positions of vantage upon every topout.

If it had been dark, he thought, at least not all the disadvantage would be with him, but last night they had been busy elsewhere — with the cattle.

It was still not daybreak as he led the Macdonalds southward in a slow lope. He had tried this before, and at least when he had been caught that time, it had been by a Bannock.

He hoped that would be the case again

— if they were captured — because it did not really matter how they reached the camp as long as they reached it.

None of them spoke much. The Macdonalds appeared to be of the opinion that the three of them were racing against a paling night.

They angled over to ride with the forest as their background. It would not fool anyone who knew what had to be acquired in order to be a good sign-reader, but Gus felt better riding this way and he was the leader.

They stopped only when the sun was half above the horizon, as much because Gus needed orientation as to rest the animals.

His best estimate was that they were now well south of the Bannock rancheria. It also happened to be the least inviting area to attempt breaching the mountains, so they went farther southward until Gus found a place that could be crossed, but not without considerable effort and long periods of rest.

He did not feel pressed for time. He was reasonably certain that after the soldiers had been scattered miles in all directions, he and his companions had plenty of time.

But it had never been soldiers that worried him. He worried about the Cheyenne.

Part of the time they led their animals because climbing was steep. Some other times they had to alter course to avoid immense rocks or thorny thickets, but each time they did this Gus put them back on what he thought would be roughly the same westerly course.

He was not exactly on course as no one else would have been who was navigating by dead reckoning and after each digression he attempted to make an appropriate correction in order to re-align himself with his objective.

The important thing was from here on to watch for Indians. Each time he led his companions around a high ridge, he did it by skirting well below the topout. If there were game trails he used them, if there were not he muddled along making corrections as he went.

They saw no Indians and had not expected to. For a fact they could have been within a hundred and fifty feet of one and as long as he did not move they would not have seen him. Most of the way they walked or rode watching the ground ahead. It was lung-pumping, sweaty work.

The higher peaks and rims invariably had game trails well below, but the rockier the terrain became the less covering shelter was available to men who were covered with sweat, felt like their lungs were afire, and who watched where they were walking in slippery, rocky places, rather than peering up and around.

They halted where a miserly little creek made dog-leg bends, and where the water was protected from discovery by thickets too thick to be cut through with machetes, which they did not have.

They lingered in this silent, hidden place. Here, Gus left the Macdonalds to scout ahead on foot. Alfred and Henry sank down, soaked bandanas then slowly squeezed them at the back of the neck. It helped, but their secret place was muggy, the sun could not penetrate to the ground in most places, but its evaporating propensity heightened the mugginess until the Macdonalds no longer cared about thirst or weariness, they just hoped Gus Ruby would return soon, which he did not do. It seemed an eternity before he clawed his way to the shady place where two men and two horses waited.

"I saw two of 'em. If we could avoid loosening rocks up the sidehill of one, I think we can grab him."

That was a remote possibility, the ground was covered with small rocks, there was precious little cover and they would have to belly-crawl nearly the entire distance to the Indians' watching place.

They discussed trying to get past. Gus shook his head about that. The alternative, then, was to retrace their way back down to level ground and ride a mile or two farther southward, which none of them were keen about, they had got this far, wasting hours all over again to possibly get farther down-country before attempting another westerly hike, was unacceptable.

Gus told the younger men the best choice was to reach one of the hidden Cheyenne, and either kill or capture him without making a sound. They would have to leave the horses in the canyon which was about the same as sailors burning their ships behind them.

Gus cleared a place and made a map in dust showing where both the Cheyenne were, then suggested that they try to take out the one farthest south. He had to guess about there being other Cheyenne still farther south, but doubted it. According to his estimate, they were already well south of the Bannock rancheria. There would be no reason for other enemies of the Bannocks to be any farther south.

They sweated their way up the slope. They had left the horses contentedly dozing, had looped their spurs around saddle horns, and only had to worry about making noise, which would not be easy; as Gus had said, there was shale rock almost all the way to the high place where the hostile was squatting.

It did not cross his mind that the Indian up there had been watching the area to the north and west since yesterday, and no man, not even seemingly tireless Cheyenne, could go without sleep forever.

The sun burned downward, thirst troubled the stalkers who were fanned out southward. Deer flies too, abounded. This was game country. Deer flies stung when they bit.

Gus crawled in the direction of a sickly bush which under other circumstances would only have reached to his knees. It was the only cover. Once he passed it there would be no cover at all until he got up to where the hostile was sitting.

He kept the bush between himself and the topout, paused to rest behind it, listened to a hammering heart, flung sweat off and looked back the way he had come. He could see for miles. The land was empty of movement. It looked enticingly attractive. He flopped over onto his stomach looking upward. There was nothing to be seen. When he had seen the hostile earlier this one had been on one knee. Now, he was evidently flat down.

The Indian farther north was in a stand of second-growth timber, leaning there. Except for moving to look back, Gus probably would not have seen that one. The distance between the two watchers was about a quarter mile, maybe a tad more.

Gus did not worry about the second Indian seeing him even though to do so all the Cheyenne had to do was stroll back far enough to see along the eastern slope.

The rancheria had to be northward, which meant Gus had led his companions much farther southward than he had intended. So much for guesswork-corrections as they had come down-country.

Once, when he paused to lie flat and suck air, it occurred to Gus that being farther southward actually was in his favour. That hostile overhead was probably as far behind the rancheria as the Cheyenne had got to encircle the Bannock camp.

He started inching upward again concentrating on the topout. There was no sign of Henry or Alfred Macdonald.

His last stop was about a hundred feet below the rim. He had got this far by stealth, the most difficult part lay ahead. If the hostile up there, for whatever reason, walked back and looked down, he would see Gus flat as a lizard below.

Gus wiped a sweaty palm, felt for

his sixgun, took several deep breaths and started worming his way the last few feet. He was less than twenty feet from the rim when a distant gunshot reverberated. Gus considered, thought the Cheyenne would be looking in the direction of that shot, and belly-crawled to within a few feet of the rim where he paused to palm his sixgun and prepare for the confrontation shortly to take place.

There was another distant gunshot, followed by a second one. Gus did not speculate, he accepted those diversions as something providence had provided, and reached for the nearest upright rock along the rim of the topout with his left hand, gripped it for a final pull, while simultaneously jockeying his right hand with the Colt in it, over the rim.

Providence or pure luck, whichever it was, favoured the crawling man. He came up over the rim of an area roughly twenty feet square, windswept down to granite, with the back of an Indian about fifteen feet in front. The hostile was tall, whittled down to bone, sinew and muscle. He had a Winchester saddle gun in his right hand. He did not appear to have a sidearm but there was a large, bone-handled fleshing knife in a rawhide scabbard at his belt.

The Cheyenne wore buckskin trousers, from which the fringe had been cut off, if there had ever been any. His shirt was faded and dirty, it was some kind of cotton, dark blue with tiny red flowers all over it. Whoever this Indian was, he showed clear evidence of an association of the races, his britches were pure Indian as his shirt was pure store boughten.

Gus stood up, pointed the gun and cocked it. The Indian did not move. Gus told him to drop the Winchester. He still did not move. Gus walked a little closer, finger curled inside the trigger guard. He ordered the hostile to turn facing him, and this time he was obeyed, but very slowly, almost as though the Cheyenne did not want to see what was behind him.

Gus had an Indian captive who understood commands in English, which was gratifying. Lately, he'd come to feel like an alien.

He ordered the Cheyenne to drop the saddle gun for the second time. This time the Indian's black eyes with their muddy whites flickered past Gus as he let the gun drop. His gaze was over Gus's right shoulder and slightly eastward.

The Indian began a slow, exultant smile. Until he did that Gus was confident that what he had been looking at behind Gus was either Henry or Alfred, or maybe both. He was wrong.

Without a sound an Indian with a lined face, a lipless mouth and keen black eyes spoke from directly behind Gus. "You throw down the gun."

Gus let out a long breath. All that damned crawling over sharp stones for nothing. He let his sixgun fall.

Ahead, the taller Indian who had until recently been Gus's prisoner, smiled, retrieved his Winchester and said something cryptic to the other hostile, whose acknowledgement was a grunt.

The larger, younger Indian walked over to Gus and stared. Gus met the steady look right up until someone on the south side of the topout and a little to the east, spoke clearly and sharply.

"Hey, broncos, shed your weapons. *Now!*"

Both Indians turned to see who had spoken. All they saw was spiky and splintered rocks on the rim pretty much like the same kind of rocks Gus had encountered as he came over the topout.

The next command came in the kind of hard, flat tones that clearly meant business. *"Shed them guns!"*

Neither Indian had to understand the language, they only had to recognise the tone of voice used. They let the weapons fall.

Gus moved closer to the west rim and a voice came up to him as though from a great distance. "We seen you, Mister. Don't get between us an' them."

Gus did not get between the Indians and the invisible speaker just out of sight below the rim. He did not think the voice belonged to either Alfred or Henry. He was as much at a loss as were the Indians.

After a while Gus said, "All right. It's safe, mister, come on up."

There was not a sound, no reply to Gus, no more commands, no sound of any kind.

During this bizarre interlude Alfred and his brother appeared at the southernmost point of the rim. They climbed up and over, paused long enough to beat flint, dirt and tiny slivers off as they appraised what they saw, two unarmed Indians, Gus holding a cocked weapon, and all three of them looking thoroughly mystified in the direction of the west rim which had the same kind of low, upthrusting rocks that the other parts of the topout had.

Gus left Henry and Alfred watching the prisoners, went over and cautiously looked down the slope.

There was not a moving thing. Gus went over where the voice had sounded and stood a long time looking for sign in that area.

When he returned the others asked what he had found. He looked each of them in the eye as he said, "Nothing," and went over to gather up weapons off the ground. He needed that much time, that much exertion, to work off the coldness he had felt peering down the empty side of their hilltop. When he returned to dump the weapons in a pile Alfred gestured. "What do we do with 'em?"

Gus examined their prisoners for the first time. They were both exemplary specimens of manhood. One was slightly shorter and older than the first bronco to be captured.

It was this shorter of the two

hostiles who eventually spoke. "We are hunters."

Gus grimaced. "Sure you are. Hunters for human beings, in this case the old gent someone shot, an' maybe others."

The older man spoke with rising expectations. "We don't always single out any particular game to kill."

Gus gazed at the younger Indian and jerked his head. "How about strong-heart here? He wasn't spyin' from up here, he was watching for game, maybe an elk or some does."

When the Indians made no further attempt to speak, they were put face down, then with their mouths gagged, arms and legs also made fast and tight, about all they could do was writhe and roll, except that their eyes were particularly notable for their expressions of venom.

Alfred went down to retrieve the horses. While he was gone Henry said, "You saw something down the slope where that voice came from."

Gus said, "Did I? Tell me what I saw."

Henry reddened, his back was to the tied Indians on the ground. After a moment during which neither he nor Gus spoke, Henry went over to look down that sidehill himself.

Gus rolled and lighted a smoke. The distant Indian among the northward trees was not visible which could indicate that he had seen something over on the more southerly topout where there were suddenly more men than there should have been, in which case he was either lying low out of sight, or had gone somewhere to warn the others that his nearest watcher might be in trouble.

When the horses arrived, rather breathless after the hike, Gus looped two lariats from the saddles of Alfred and Henry around the necks of the Cheyenne, handed each Macdonald the tag end of the rope, and did not mount his horse but instead led down into a swale and up the other side in the direction of those trees where he had seen the other sentinel. He led his animal the full distance, got into the trees, saw plenty of sign but found no Indian.

From this spot they could look up a wide place between mountains where the Bannock encampment had been. There was nothing down there, no people, no animals, no sign that the place had been inhabited except for numerous brush shelters. Gus tied his horse before asking the captured Indians how long they had known the rancheria had been abandoned. The Indians glared and said nothing. Gus walked over to the youngest buck and poked him in the middle of the chest as he repeated the question. This time when he got no answer Alfred Macdonald leaned from the saddle holding a big, heavy fleshing knife butt first. Gus took the weapon and went back to face the Indian. It was the same knife Gus had seen this same Indian carrying.

He rested the point against the Indian's soft parts. The older and shorter hostile said something guttural and crisp. The younger one spoke. "They left the camp two days ago." He jutted his jaw. "That way."

"Men?"

"No, old people, young ones, women with pack animals."

Alfred spoke angrily. "He's lying. Look down there. Even from up here you can see they took the same trail we've always used to get in here."

Gus went to the edge of the timber. Sure enough, the evidence of many people and animals went northward on that cork-screw wide trail he had used to reach the camp days back.

He returned to the prisoners. "That's what those gunshots were about," he said, making a question of it. "Cheyenne saw some stragglers, maybe some old people who could not keep up."

The shorter, older Indian spoke. "No. The people were gone. They got away in the night before we were all in place. We heard them, but they were already near the end of that trail, near the open country. The shooting," the Indian paused to squint northward. "There were many Bannock men behind in ambushes, on peaks, among trees and rocks. When we could see down there they were hidden but we knew they were there." The older man suddenly stopped to expectorate spitefully. "We did not know — the army was supposed to be waiting when they came out of the mountains . . . There was no army. We waited but nothing happened. A rider came to tell us something about cattle charging into the soldiers and they would not be out there to meet the Bannocks."

The older bronco was bitter. "We were not enough so we waited in here because we thought some of the Bannocks would come back. We could have beaten fifteen, maybe fifty, so we waited. We came a long way to fight

Bannocks . . . They got away."

Gus pieced things together, made sense out of what he had heard and pointed the big knife at the older bronco. "Can they hear you from here?"

"Who?" the bitter Indian asked.

"Your friends, the other Cheyenne."

The old man showed his teeth when he replied angrily. "There is no one to hear us. There was a man here among these trees. There were others waiting. We decided last night if the soldiers did not arrive, we would quit and go back as soon as the sun was overhead."

Gus looked up. The sun had not been directly overhead for at least two hours. He looked at the older Cheyenne again. "Go back — where?"

"To the fort to get our pay. We did what the army wanted us to do. It was not our fault the Bannocks got away, it was the army's fault."

Gus saw Alfred and Henry watching him. He shrugged at them, stuck the big knife in his belt and pointed downward.

The old Indian jutted his jaw. "Ahead there is a deer trail to go down."

Gus finally mounted to lead off. Behind him Alfred and Henry were ready in an instant to set up their horses and yank the ropes taut whose slip-knots were around the captive Cheyenne.

They wanted to ask about their father. Gus had wondered about that too, but until they got off the rims, down into the trail, no one could lope back to make certain George Macdonald was back in that brush shelter.

He wasn't and by the time Gus got to the trail below he was ready to believe the Bannock would not abandon their benefactor.

11

Up to their Hocks

WHEN they were on the canyon floor with high mountains on both sides Alfred handed Gus the tag-end of the rope he had been carrying, at the noose-end of which was the big young Cheyenne, turned and rode back to search the abandoned rancheria.

Gus expected Cheyenne. The canyon was an ideal place for an ambush. He told the captives that if they saw any broncos, either Cheyenne or Bannock, they were to yell to them not to shoot.

It was not something a mounted man among men afoot would ordinarily want to wager his life on, but there was no alternative except to go yard by yard looking for bushwhackers, which Gus had no intention of doing.

The shorter of the captives made a sneering remark to Gus. "You afraid of shadows? There are no Cheyenne up here now. They will be trailing the Bannock miles ahead. Maybe with the army." Gus rolled and lighted a smoke for supper, ignored the Cheyenne and with Henry, scanned every bush, every rock, every canyon shadow looking for movement or reflecting light.

It was a long walk. There was no way to make haste as long as they had those Cheyenne on foot. Alfred returned as the others were passing over into the easterly canyon where that washed-out place was. He had not found his father. He had searched the village. There was one Bannock, a sturdy dark woman sitting alone in a brush shelter. She met Alfred with a cocked Winchester. He walked into her brush shelter and she had commanded him to stop and keep his hands in her sight. Alfred shook his head. She was sweaty and ugly.

Gus had a flash of intuition. "Did her voice sound familiar, Alfred?"

Young Macdonald rode several yards before replying. "For a fact, it did."

"Sort of rough and deep?"

Instead of answering the question Alfred sat straight up in his saddle. *"It was her!"*

Henry gave his brother a baffled look. "Her — what?" "It was her — the same voice — that was just below the rim and told those Indians to drop their guns. Hell, no wonder she was sweaty, she'd climbed that hillside and went back down it."

Gus smiled to himself. He remembered the woman's smile when he had gone back for a refill of his bowl. He also recalled something else: That woman and another saying something back and forth in their own language, then laughing.

What he could not understand was why she had remained behind when the others had left. If a Cheyenne had found her she would have been killed.

Gus stubbed out his smoke. *Someone* would have been killed. If she had been sitting in a dark brush shelter, a Cheyenne poking his head might have never lived to see another sunrise.

Why?

The Bannock were friends of the Macdonalds. She would not have shot Alfred, but why had she hung back? Whatever the reason it had to be a good one; she knew what would happen to her if a Cheyenne found her alone back there.

Henry interrupted Gus's reverie. He was pointing with an upraised arm. Gus, his brother and the Cheyenne also looked up.

There was an Indian above them on a rough, flat place on the west side of the canyon. He was holding a Winchester in both hands watching. Gus decided that if the Indian had intended to shoot, he could have done it any time since the little cavalcade had begun its last long trek toward open country.

The Cheyenne held a brief discussion, lowered their faces and trudged along. Whatever they had said evidently had to do with the possibility of the Indian atop the high place being hostile.

They plodded past. The last Gus saw of the Indian sentinel was just before the watcher turned down the far side of his vantage point.

A few hundred more yards they met two Bannock with a battered Cheyenne between them. They were ahorseback, their captive was afoot. Gus did not recognise either of the Bannock. Henry and Alfred knew them, though. There was a short discussion before Henry told the Bannock to go ahead with their prisoner. As they rode off the prisoner, a rope around his neck, his hands tied in front, looked hard at the other pair of Cheyenne. Not a word was spoken until the Indian captive trotted ahead to keep up with his captors, then the young bronco spoke to his companion whose answer sounded scornful.

Gus kept the lead with the mounted

Bannock well ahead. The closer they got to open country the less he worried about an ambush. The moment they passed the crags on both sides sunshine hit them. The land looked empty. The older warrior told Henry where a sump-spring was and said he was thirsty. Henry would have assented to the diversion but Alfred wouldn't. He growled at the Cheyenne, flicked slack in the rope, the Indian faced forward and continued to follow the rump of Gus's horse.

When they were easing easterly, travelling farther from the mountains, one of the Bannock spoke quickly to his companion and loped ahead, but angling toward the wooded sidehills so he would be somewhat concealed.

Gus called a halt. Alfred said, "He saw something up ahead. He's gone to scout it up."

They dismounted to wait in horse-shade. The young Cheyenne sank to the ground refusing to look at any of the others, even his fellow tribesman, who muttered something which the younger buck ignored.

It was a long wait, Gus was impatient. He did not anticipate any trouble. At least if any appeared they would be able to see it long before it got close. He felt sure what the older bronco had said about the Cheyenne being disgusted when the army did not show up, and having withdrawn was correct.

With no real basis for the conviction he was sure that bronco they had seen spying on them from a high place had been a Bannock.

He was correct but it would be a long time before his hunch was proven correct.

The old bronco did not say another word about thirst, which was just as well. No one would have heeded him.

There was heat in the day. What prevented it from being worse than it was, could be attributed to a high, thin veil-like overcast which did not obscure the sun but which diffused and neutralised it. That kind of an overcast usually meant rain was on the way. In this respect Idaho was no different from most other places.

The Bannock returned, dropped to the ground, let one rein drag, kept the other one in his fist and spoke to Alfred. Their discussion was prolonged before Alfred interpreted for Gus. "There's dust cloud ahead some distance. It's not the army. It's going north, not coming toward us."

Gus said, "Bannock on the move?"

The bronco had not got that close. Alfred said as much and looked puzzled. "It could be, but under these circumstances with Cheyenne maybe shagging them, an' the army maybe coming down-country. I don't think the Bannock would be in open country. They was supposed to herd their women an' children to another rancheria miles west through the mountains."

The older Cheyenne spoke sourly. "They run out of mountains."

No one heeded that remark. In Idaho

no one ran out of mountains.

Gus asked Alfred who the makers of dust could be. He got a bewildered shake of the head for an answer.

They could not dawdle where they were so Gus led off on a slanting route that would take them northward but also far enough easterly to reach the Macdonald yard. After that, he had no idea.

The army would be in the saddle again soon. By now the colonel had probably sent for reinforcements. Otherwise, by now residents of that distant town would have heard enough rumours to put another mounted force, possibly vigilantes or possemen, in the area.

What created a difficulty for Gus was that he had no idea when these things would happen, or even how they would happen.

He kept a dead reckoning on the ranch yard until he had rooftops in sight, then Henry rode up beside him to say, "I'll scout. If we go back to the yard someone will see us there sooner or later. We've lost track of what's going on."

Gus could have agreed with the last of that statement, for a fact events had for some inexplicable reason, passed them by.

He warned Henry to be careful, watched the youngest Macdonald ride away, continued his course toward the yard while at the same time seeking other banners of dust, or any movement at all that could have been either a threat or a benefit.

Gus saw nothing. The land was soft-toned by that high overcast, it seemed as endlessly indifferent as it must have seemed since the beginning of time.

They reached the yard where the older bronco finally got his drink at the stone trough out back. He and the other Cheyenne were then taken into the barn and chained to massive log uprights while Alfred and Gus moved out of earshot and Gus spoke as he rolled a smoke.

"What bothers me is what's become of your paw."

Alfred answered easily. "They took him with them."

"He wasn't in no shape to travel. The woman who was tending him said he'd start bleedin' the moment they put him on a horse."

One of the prisoners called from inside the barn. Alfred turned away leaving Gus with more riddles than he thought there would be explanations to. He smoked, squinted over where that dust had been, and saw that it had passed farther northward, but two horsemen were approaching from roughly the same direction. When they reached the yard Gus recognised the two rangemen that had been left in the yard when he and the Macdonalds had ridden south.

Art Headley dismounted a trifle stiffly, something which happened to older riders in any kind of chilly weather, day or night. Will Stratton led their horses toward the barn and stopped stone still when he heard someone in there speaking in a language he did not understand. Alfred sitting on the ground with two Bannock and three other Indians.

Behind him Headley told Gus come daybreak they had seen dust west of the yard a few miles and rode to investigate.

"We got about half way when four fellers seen us and stopped. We decided the dust could wait, rode back where them gents in their button shoes an' little curly-brim hats was as still as moles. I figured they'd ask about the dust. Instead they said they wanted to talk to George Macdonald. Will said he wasn't around. They wanted to know how long he might be gone. I told 'em maybe two days, maybe two weeks, that we rode for him an' hadn't see him for some days.

"The thickest of them boys, a bearded feller with grey showin' from under that silly little town-hat, said he was a Deputy U.S. Marshal, an' wanted to know if Mister Macdonald had anyone at the house he could talk to.

"I told him Mister Macdonald didn't have no wife, an' his two sons was out on the range somewhere, but if he wanted, I'd be right proud to tell Mister Macdonald what the lawman wanted to see him about an' that maybe, if I knew where the lawman was stayin' Mister Macdonald could ride over an' see him."

"Did he say what he wanted?" Gus asked.

The squinty-eyed rangeman hooked both hands in his shellbelt when he replied. "He said he was out here by order of the fer'al government to find out what part Mister Macdonald had taken in gettin' the Bannock to go off the reservation. He said he was stayin' at Fort Taylor, an' the second I seen Mister Macdonald, to tell him the marshal would be obliged if he'd pay him a call at the fort."

Gus turned in time to see Alfred

standing nearby listening. Headley waited a moment, and when nothing more was said, headed for the barn.

Alfred's anger was in place which did not surprise Gus. Alfred's anger was never far from the surface. "Paw never had no idea the Bannock was off the reservation until he met some an' they told him they had to hunt meat because their women an' children was starving."

Gus said nothing; he had heard this before, but even if he hadn't, the presence of a federal lawman in the area was nothing to be taken lightly.

He said, "I think we better find your paw."

Alfred's reply made Gus's eyes spring wide open. "He's with the Bannock. They got him fitted out in a horse-hammock."

Gus thought of what that Shoshoni school marm had told him. But all he said was, "Where?"

"On their way back to the reservation," Alfred replied, and added a little more.

"I think that's what was below that dust we saw travellin' north. In the barn just now I asked the Cheyenne which way they figured the Bannock had gone. They said west, deeper into the mountains, an' the Bannock laughed at them. They told me they knew the army's hired In'ians was watchin' everythin' they did, so they parted, most of 'em doin' exactly that — goin' deeper into the mountains in the dark. He said their racket was deliberate. It give the band with paw a chance to get back down out of there in the dark, which is what they did, travellin' slow an' bein' as quiet as they could.

"Them Cheyenne didn't like that. They're supposed to be the best sign readers in the country. They said no root-eatin' damned Bannock could escape when they was watchin' from every topout. One of the Bannock told the Cheyenne in English they wasn't the only In'ians who'd figured out ways to hide from enemies. The Cheyenne said the army would find that band with paw."

Gus had listened while leaning on the tie-rack with both arms folded across his chest. He stepped away from the man in front of him to look for the banner of dust. It was visible, but just barely. The Bannock with Macdonald were not wasting any time.

Gus asked how far it was to the reservation. Alfred held up two fingers.

Gus wagged his head. "The army's stirred up," he said. "If we saw dust so will the army's scouts. If they figure that Bannock are goin' back to the reservation, my guess is that they'll do exactly what they did with the Nez Perce, they won't try to overtake them, they'll ride hard to get ahead of them, make a battle line across the route of the Bannock, and most likely force a fight. Alfred, I think Mister Donavon has to whip them or he's not goin' to come out of this mess lookin' very good, and army officers got to look good."

"What about the In'ians? They'll look good if they get back to the reservation before the colonel — "

"It won't happen, Alfred. General Miles set the precedent; you got to beat the In'ians in the field, beat them down to their knees even though they are tired, hungry, whipped already."

For a moment neither man spoke, then Alfred said, "I'll find them, tell them what's ahead and go back into the mountains with them."

Gus nodded solemnly, he had expected Alfred to say something like that. "Good luck, partner. They got one hell of a head start on you."

Alfred stared. "You don't want to come?"

"Alfred, I worked for the army for a lot of years. There aren't any In'ians left strong enough to whip soldiers. I expect they'll go on tryin' until some war leaders, some spokesman, convinces 'em all they're goin' to do is the same as the Kiowas done — fight themselves out of existence."

Alfred's dark eyes narrowed. "You want that to happen!"

"No, I don't want that to happen. What kind of a damfool thing is that for you to say to me. I've been bustin' my buttons ever since this fandango began to help you folks an' your In'ians."

Alfred said no more, he even relaxed a little as they looked at each other. Eventually Gus said, "Alfred, when you can't out-fight someone, you got to out-smart 'em."

"How?"

"First off, you'n your brother forget the Bannocks out yonder with your paw. You ride straight to the reservation an' tell the agent the Indians are comin' in. For him to pass that along to the army. Tell him to do whatever he can to keep the soldiers away, let his In'ians come back where he thinks they belong."

"What will you be doing?"

Gus smiled thinly. "Me, Henry, Will and Art will be doin' what you wanted to do. Catch up with them In'ians and if your paw's with them sound him out on an idea I got."

"What idea?"

"Alfred, if you got two days of ridin' ahead of you, you'd better get started . . . One more thing you can do: Get the In'ian agent to ride back south with you to meet the reservation jumpers."

"To use his authority to keep the soldiers away?"

Gus's thin smile lingered. "Yes. If he can. If he can't there's goin' to be one hell of a fight. Impress that on him, then, when he's got that settled with Mister Donavon, you'n Mister Agent ride south until we meet you."

Alfred did not move. Gus stopped smiling. "You can trust me, or you can trust the army an' its Cheyenne. That way we can both predict what will happen. My way, whether it works or not, it'll keep the soldiers away from the In'ians. They'll have a chance. Get a fresh horse, Alfred, a real stout one. You got a lot of ridin' to do."

12

A Time of Tears

TIRED men left the Macdonald yard, Henry, Gus, and Art Headley. Stratton remained behind with one Bannock to watch the prisoners. The other Bannock also remained behind, but to rest their animals, then they told Gus, they would track after him.

They did not ride fast for an hour, or until their animals were thoroughly warmed out, then they loped. There was no sign of Alfred.

The day was well advanced, that softly obscuring veil remained overhead, they saw cattle in little bands but not until the ranch yard was no longer in sight.

Henry had questions to which Gus had no answers, only speculations.

When Henry asked specifically what plan Gus had in mind, the older man smiled at Henry and rode in silence.

When they cut the sign of many unshod horses going north, they eased their animals out to close as much of the distance as possible.

It was a long, tedious ride. If they had been fresh it would still have been that kind of a ride. The freshest man among them was the squinty-eyed rangeman named Headley. He was never very talkative. On this ride he did not say a word unless he was addressed then he gave minimal answers.

They found an abandoned horse. It was an old, sway-backed animal with age-spaces between the ribs which made Gus estimate its age at about twenty. The horse was peacefully cropping grass of which there was an abundance, but as he chewed small round tufts of wet grass came out the side of his mouth. The reason was basic, the older a horse got the more of his grinding teeth loosened and fell out. An old horse with few grinders left, or none, could stand up to his belly in the finest most nourishing grass and still starve to death.

The old horse eyed them with little interest. They viewed him only because he was the first sign of living evidence of what was still miles ahead.

They were still riding with dusk settling when someone fired a gun from a great distance, so great in fact that the sound arrived as more of a reverberating, faint shock wave than an actual sound. They rode with all attention forward. If there were more shots it could possibly mean the army had already caught up with the Bannocks.

No second or third shot followed. Gus said, "A pot hunter." Art agreed but added a little more, "Better to go hungry for another day than to maybe be heard by someone from Fort Taylor."

Right or wrong, and Gus nodded slightly in agreement, the shot *had* been fired. Nothing more was said. An hour later they were roughly parallel with Fort Taylor, but a considerable distance west. They were alert; if Colonel Donavon had scouts out, this was most likely the countryside they would be ranging across.

They saw no one, but they wouldn't have anyway unless they met a scout face to face. Nightfall was taking the place of dusk.

Because they had made good time Gus halted for a short rest. He and Henry were still carrying those cloth-wrapped bundles of food. The three of them ate what would ordinarily have been food to avoid because of its greasy sogginess, but hunger, particularly the kind that had not been appeased in a long time, could be satisfactorily taken care of by just about anything that would go down, and stay down.

Afterwards, when Gus rolled a smoke and Art Headley tucked a chew into his cheek, Henry asked for the hundredth time how all this was going to turn out, and Gus, who had gone over the same ground so many times lately he was not very interested in mere speculation, said very little. As they were snugging up to continue the race to catch up, Art Headley made a dry comment.

"About like all these kinds of stunts turn out, except that this time it's whites tryin' to save In'ians from other whites."

They thought, because the Indians would stop for the night with guards out all around, they might close the distance better if they did not stop again, nor did they.

The toll was harder on the men than on the horses, which had been favoured and which had been eating, sleeping and resting until Gus and his companions returned to the yard with the captives.

Art Headley was a shrewd man in his quiet way. He wondered aloud about the Bannock back at the yard who had not been around when he, Gus and Henry had struck out.

As a subject worth discussing it had little to commend it and Art let it die when all he got from his companions was grunts.

Gus dozed in the saddle, as did Art. Henry should have, he'd been as long without rest as the others, but he was also a good bit younger. He watched that his companions did not fall from their saddles, which they did not do, and he also gauged the night as they rode through it.

It was Henry who eventually jarred Gus and Art awake. He had smelled smoke. The three of them raised their plodding animals into a lope and held to this gait until there was no question about it, the scent of smoke was in the night, and not just smoke, the scent of cooking.

They were close and so was dawn. Gus was hesitant about approaching the Bannock camp until dawn arrived. Art nodded about that and Henry did not disagree but would probably have ridden into the camp if the others had decided not to.

They walked another half a mile, until Art told Gus quietly, that sentinels with itching trigger fingers had to be close, then they halted, dismounted, hobbled their saddled animals, draped bridles from saddle horns and sat down.

Within moments both Gus and Henry were asleep. Art Headley got a fresh cud into his cheek, eyed the sleeping men and shook his head. No one was ever going to believe he and the other two had ridden their behinds raw to save some Indians. Things like that simply did not happen in the age, and the time, Art was living through.

He arose to look at the horses, and met an armed Indian face to face in the moonless night. It was a chilling, completely unexpected confrontation. The Indian was about Art's size and heft. He was holding an old Winchester in both hands aiming at the white man's middle. Art, who knew no Bannock, tried English even though he knew English-speaking Indians in the northwest were more scarce than almost anywhere else.

"Friend," he said, and jerked a thumb. "Henry Macdonald is sleepin' over yonder. The other feller is called Gus. We rode hard to catch up. We want to talk to George Macdonald."

The Indian remained blank-faced. Art sighed, turned slightly and called Henry, who was deeply asleep and softly snoring. The Indian never once moved his Winchester so that it wasn't aimed, but he stepped past, saw Henry and Gus, looked at Art and said something that might as well have been Greek to Headley.

Art resolved the dilemma by walking close to shake Henry awake. For almost half a minute after awakening Henry rubbed his eyes, saw the armed Indian, rubbed some more and finally came up off the ground. He spoke and the Indian answered. Both of them launched into a conversation where interrupting each other appeared to be part of the process.

Headley, meanwhile awakened Gus who sat up, looked, listened then grudgingly got to his feet. Henry addressed Gus in English. "The camp's yonder, maybe half a mile. This Bannock's part of the night-watch."

Gus absorbed that and asked a question for Henry to interpret into Bannock. He said, "Is George Macdonald alive?" and scarcely breathed while awaiting the reply.

Henry eventually nodded and smiled. "He's alive."

Gus loosened all over, his plan depended upon the elder Macdonald being alive. He told Henry to tell the Bannock they would now get their horses and ride into the camp.

The Indian, leaning on his Winchester, appeared to have no objection. He stood slightly apart as they brought the animals in to be bitted. They were already saddled.

As they mounted the Indian went

ahead of them. He trotted so their horses had to do the same to keep up. They passed among unkempt, hurried, blanket camps, saw a few fires, a number of Bannock standing like statues watching riders pass being led by the Indian.

Where the bronco halted and gestured someone had created a passable brush shelter, nothing that would survive the first hard wind, but by that time of year the Bannock would not be down here.

The Bannock took their reins before they ducked into the brush shelter where a single candle burned. Visibility was hindered, each time someone moved rolling the air, the candle wavered.

A willowy woman of indeterminate years, but young enough to be supple as she came up to her feet, faced the rumpled, unshaven men without speaking. Behind her on a thick pallet of buffalo robes, George Macdonald was soundly sleeping.

Henry went the closest. He asked the

woman in Bannock the condition of his father. She replied in flawless English.

"He made the trip better than I expected, but the people were very careful of him. They see in him their best chance to end this trouble without a massacre." She looked down at the sleeping man, then looked at Gus. Of course she recognised him but her face showed nothing as she said, "Scouts saw soldiers."

"Where?"

"Back at that fort they made of logs."

Gus's relief was obvious even in the poor light. He jutted his jaw downward. "Waken him, we got to talk."

The Shoshoni school teacher did not move. "He was very tired. I fed him broth. He needs all the rest he can get."

"The wound didn't break loose?"

"Only once, a small tear, when he tried to raise up and look around." She looked down. "He is the only white man I ever saw, except preachers, who try very hard to help Indians . . . And the preachers stay in their homes and pray, which doesn't turn bullets or provide food. He will recover. He is tough and . . . "

"And?"

She looked straight at George. "And he belongs, his wife was Bannock."

Gus jerked a thumb. "This is Henry Macdonald the son of the Bannock woman."

The school teacher glanced at Henry, who smiled, turned back toward Gus and asked if the soldiers were coming. He thought they were, if not this night then surely within the next few days.

She asked if George Macdonald being with the tribesmen would stop the army.

This time it was Art Headley who replied. As usual he was straight-forward. "The federal law wants Mister Macdonald. He's supposed to have got the In'ians to leave the reservation — something like that. If the federal marshal comes with the soldiers . . . I

221

don't know. Havin' Mister Macdonald here might be worse for you folks. A federal warrant, and soldiers, mean trouble, lady. Nothing I can think of will prevent it."

Gus cut in. He had seen the tightening of the handsome Shoshoni's face. He did not want her to sound the alarm for battle. Not just yet anyway. He sank to one knee and gently jostled George Macdonald.

The woman looked strongly disapproving. He had been her responsibility through harrowing experiences, she felt responsible for him.

Henry watched his father awaken, scowl at Gus until he recognised him, then his face cleared as Gus began to talk.

They all listened. George Macdonald was no more intent than were Art and Henry. Even the Shoshoni woman listened carefully.

When Gus stopped talking George Macdonald held up a hand to the woman. "I got to have a piece of paper an somethin' to write with."

When she left the brush shelter two Indians came inside and placed themselves on each side of the opening, clearly guards. Henry spoke to one of them. They knew each other. The Indian answered quietly but did not smile.

When the woman returned she had an old man with her. George Macdonald spoke to him in Bannock. He listened with considerable gravity, then departed without a glance at Gus, Art or Henry.

Gus would have asked Henry what had been said but the Shoshoni woman scattered his thought. "We will move him," she told the others. "He wants to be taken to the edge of camp where he can see what happens."

Dawn chill was in the air when those two burly Bannock by the entranceway responded to the woman's statement in their language, which Henry understood perfectly and gestured for Gus and Art to stand clear.

The Indians picked up Macdonald's bearskin pallet as though it were weightless and carried him outside where the first bluish streaks of a new day were visible. The camp was smoky, people called back and forth, women hunkered near fire rings, and for the second time Gus stood in the midst of a Bannock camp, but this one contained old men, women and children, there were few fighting age bucks nowhere nearly as many as there normally would have been.

Indians watched as the buffalo robe pallet was carried past. No one made a sound, even children were silent as the pallet and its burden were well past heading toward the southern end of the camp.

Gus told Henry and Art to get the horses, they had some riding to do. When they were astride Henry hesitated before passing his father's pallet, called something in Bannock and raised his right arm. The wounded man smiled but only raised his hand

224

to return the salute. He did not say a word until the riders were beyond the camp, then he told the Shoshoni woman in English that his youngest son favoured his Bannock mother.

The woman was watching Gus and nodded only absently. When the riders were no longer in sight she knelt to examine her patient. There was no fresh bleeding. She rocked back on her heels and asked if Gus's plan would work.

Macdonald only smiled at her. He had watched his youngest son out of sight. He reminded Macdonald of his wife. It was a bitter-sweet moment.

The Bannock only knew that something was in the air. No one told them and they did not speculate very much. They were less than three miles from the reservation, which normally would have meant sanctuary for them, but under the present circumstances they were not convinced they would be safe when they got there. It was a bad time for them, they faced it with misgivings, they had heard of massacres by soldiers.

Only one man stood between them and bloodletting. He had convinced them to return to the reservation and they had come, but every mile they got closer, the harder it was for them to believe they would be safe.

Stories of soldiers going into reservations to kill people were rare, but soldiers *did* kill Indians.

Their old men conferred while the smoke rose, children ran, dogs barked and women cooked over deadfall fires. They had discussed all the options many times. There was really little to say which was fresh, and all things considered the problem remained the same. If they reached the reservation ahead of the soldiers, at least they would be back on their allotted land. But it was the unknown, the part of their punishment for leaving in the first place, which worried them.

Two old men went to sit beside George Macdonald's pallet in stoic silence. He and they watched the sun arrive, saw miles of empty land; began to hope that, for some reason, the army had turned back. At least they saw no sign of soldiers in the newday light, which was encouraging. They smiled a little and Macdonald smiled back.

A Bannock fighting man came into camp from the west where he had been keeping watch from a high place. He rode his horse down where Macdonald and the old men were sitting, raised a bronzed arm and gestured. In Bannock he said, "You watch in the wrong direction. They are not out there, they are behind us, a double line of them, horse soldiers and foot soldiers."

The old man stared at the messenger, looked around at Macdonald and one of them spoke Bannock. "Behind us; between us and the reservation? The same way they caught the Nez Perce."

Macdonald spoke harshly at them. "Pick me up, carry me back where I can see them and they can see me."

227

The old man departed fatalistically resigned, as other Indians picked up the pallet and started back with it through the smoky camp, which had somehow understood that all was not well and watched as the white man was carried past.

The Shoshoni woman walked beside the pallet, expressionless and dry-eyed. Somewhere southward their three helpers were riding in the wrong direction. She leaned, took Macdonald's hand and clung to it. He had almost got himself killed trying to save the Bannock. For a while she had felt that he might be sufficiently influential among the whites to accomplish his purpose. Now, walking beside him holding his hand, she felt that the forces arrayed against Macdonald and the Bannock had been too great.

13

Showdown

ART Headley and Gus made a mile deep sweep south and east, picked up a fair number of Macdonald cattle and were driving them when Henry returned on a lathered horse to report what his father and the Bannock already knew; the army was between the reservation and the Indians.

Art squinted at Henry harder than ever. Gus sagged in the saddle, but recovered quickly. He left Art and Henry to drive the cattle, gave them specific instructions how this was to be done, and loped away northward.

He was weary enough to drop to the ground and not arise until the end of Time. What kept him going was that, although he had not anticipated the army making a forced march, probably through the night, he *had* anticipated some variety of unpleasantness near or on the reservation.

He passed the Bannock camp less than a mile south. Smoke, distance-muted noise and ground-hugging makeshift shelters were barely visible and audible as he rode past.

Somewhere within the next few miles he expected to see blue uniforms and army wagons. The morning was clear, that overcast veil was gone. Distant mountains looked miles closer than they were, and eventually Gus saw smoke from more cooking fires. He angled a little more northwesterly until he saw wagons upon whose canvas covers were painted the crossed muskets of Donavon's infantry.

He drew to a halt looking elsewhere. Everything now depended upon Alfred, the success of his mission, and one hell of a load of luck.

The soldiers saw him sitting out there alone. There was a slight rustle of activity around a particular wagon. Two mounted civilians rode toward Gus. Behind them dragoons were readying their horses.

Gus dismounted, built and lit a smoke and waited. This was no part of his plan, but since the skyline was empty in the direction he had looked hardest, killing time might help. It surely could not hurt. Any delay was welcome.

When the pair of mounted civilians were close enough each raised a hand, palm forward. Gus responded the same way.

When they were close enough to draw rein they studied Gus and he studied them. Art Headley would have recognised the man with the face feathers who introduced himself as Deputy U.S. Marshal Hector Greenfield. The man with him was Angus Scott, a civilian interpreter for the army.

Gus acknowledged the introductions with a nod and told them who he was. Then he smoked, eyed them and waited.

Marshal Greenfield asked what he was doing out here. Gus replied as he dropped the quirley and ground it underfoot. "Me'n some other fellers are drivin' beef to the reservation."

The interpreter looked suspicious. "I never heard of the gov'ment or the army contracting for no beef for the In'ians."

Gus smiled disarmingly at the scowling interpreter. "Most likely you didn't, friend. The government nor the army had anythin' to do with this transaction."

Both men sitting their horses looking down at Gus showed no expression. "Maybe you'd ought to explain," Marshal Greenfield said.

Before speaking Gus looked northward, and this time he saw what he had been hoping very hard he would see, a party of mounted men. He had to hope with all his heart and soul it would be Alfred Macdonald bringing the Indian agent.

He faced the bleak-faced mounted

men and gestured. "Get down, gents. It's hard on a standin' horse to have all that weight on his back."

Marshal Greenfield, a man with a temper, reddened as he leaned on his saddlehorn and glared. "Mister, we'll get down when we want to. You . . . if you don't explain what you're doing out here I'll haul you back to be chained to an army wagon."

Gus did not smile. He was tempted to challenge the lawman. Instead he turned to watch those oncoming riders alter course as though to ride to the army camp. Then he smiled, straightened up and fished in a pocket as he said, "Marshal, did you ever hear of a man named George Macdonald? Well, look at this paper. In case it ain't clear to you, the Macdonald mark on cattle is a triangle with an M in the middle."

For five minutes the two unsmiling men studied the paper before Gus held up his hand to take it back. He did not get it back. Marshal

Greenfield tucked it into a pocket, his eyes cold.

"How do we know this ain't a forgery, Mister Ruby?"

Gus raised his arm. "He's over yonder in the Bannock camp. I'll take you over so you can talk to him yourself."

The mounted men exchanged a look, twisted to stare back where Indians seemed to be everywhere amid fading smoke. The interpreter shook his head. "No white man in his right mind'd ride into a camp of hostiles."

Gus disagreed. "I been with them a lot lately. So have other white men. Mister Macdonald is hurt, shot by someone — most likely an army Cheyenne — but he's able to sit up and talk. You gents want to follow me? The In'ians won't bother you, unless you upset them."

The interpreter shook his head. "No sir. I know In'ians, mister, I never go among hostiles on the prod."

Gus looked at the interpreter. "There

are mostly women and kids an' old folks."

The interpreter surprised Gus. "Maybe you're ignorant, an' maybe you want us to be first blood; army scouts been watching. Bannock warriors have been comin' into that camp all morning."

Gus turned his attention to the federal officer. "You got the note. It's genuine. I got cattle to drive so you can take the note back to Mister Donavon and — "

"*Colonel* Donavon!"

" . . . Show it to him, then set down, the whole bunch of you, because there ain't goin' to be no fight here, unless you force it, and Marshal, if you start it I give you my word I'll look for you when the shootin' starts . . . Somethin' you might pass along to the colonel. To my lights, everythin' is fair an' legal."

Gus swung astride, put a long look over where a number of men, uniformed and in civilian attire, were in what seemed to be very earnest conversation.

He loped back to find Art and Henry, never once looked back to watch the pair of grim-faced men who had his note riding at a steady walk back to the army camp.

Henry and Art were driving the cattle slowly. It had been Art's idea to move slowly because so far, although they knew what they had to do, there were some imponderables and Art Headley was a cautious individual.

When Gus joined them they began to angle the drive a little northwesterly. They raised dust even at a slow walk, which was unavoidable, and they took their time knowing that soon now the Bannocks and their opponents would see the drive.

Gus rolled a quirley with both reins looped, trickled smoke, tipped his hat brim down and watched. First, he saw Indians; they were not as disciplined as soldiers, they came to the east side of the camp, many more than Gus had seen earlier, which supported what that army interpreter had said; the broncos who had been riding in a big war party and perhaps not understanding what was happening elsewhere, had decided to return to the camp, assuming correctly that if there was to be a fight it would be there.

They had certainly seen the army scattered across the route to the reservation. As the drovers watched, a single Indian broke clear in a lope heading in their direction. Gus remembered him from the trio who had captured the Cheyenne. He raised a hand, the oncoming Bannock did the same. Gus, Art and Henry stopped. The cattle would trudge another few yards before they realised no one was pushing them, then they would begin to forage.

The Indian reined up near Henry and spoke swiftly to him. Henry nodded and interpreted. "He said the agent is with your paw. Him, an' a couple of his reservation aides. He says there was a bad argument between the army an' the agent. They want you to come."

Gus winked at Art, turned to ride back with the Bannock, and Art drily told Henry they would just let the cattle rest for a spell.

There did not appear too much activity in the soldier blockade. Some troopers who had been ordered to saddle up, were now evidently standing down.

By the time Gus got to the north edge of the Bannock camp he saw something that chilled him. Soldiers had been detailed all along the west sidehills overlooking the Indian encampment. At the same side of the camp Bannock warriors were arrayed too. Gus shook his head; one nervous tomfool who might fire a gun would precipitate a battle.

He left his horse with the Bannock messenger, moved in where a sun-shelter had been cobbled together where George Macdonald, several solemn Indian oldsters and three men Gus had never seen before were waiting.

Macdonald made the introductions.

The Shoshoni woman was beside Macdonald's pallet looking worried. She met Gus's glance and looked away.

Two of the civilians in baggy trousers and crumpled coats left whatever was to be said to the sturdily-built older man who was the agent. His name was Revelton and he wasted no time.

"The first thing, Mister Ruby, is that I got no authority to pay for them cattle. There's a process that's got to be gone through before cattle're bought for the Bannock. I requisition on the gov'ment, it maybe approves an' bucks the authority back to me an' I — "

Macdonald interrupted looking and sounding irritable. "I already told you, Mister Revelton, the cattle been bought an' paid for. They belong to the In'ians."

"You didn't tell me who bought an' paid for them," the agent exclaimed, and that seemed to inflame Macdonald further. He started to raise his voice when the Shoshoni woman placed a light hand on his shoulder. He might have ignored that or shaken the hand off, but Gus seized the initiative without raising his voice.

"Did Mister Donavon show you the bill of sale?"

The agent nodded curtly and would have spoken but Gus beat him to it. "Did Mister Macdonald verify it's his signature on the bill of sale?"

"Yes, he did, but — "

"No time for 'buts', Mister Revelton. You got hungry Indians, they got title to the cattle — it's all wrote out on that bill of sale. The army's blockin' them from drivin' their cattle onto their reservation, which they're tryin' to peacefully return to. Mister Revelton, there's a federal lawman over yonder. If you got the authority to keep outsiders from interferin' with Indian affairs . . . We're goin' to drive those cattle between this camp and the army's camp, if you got to invoke the law an' have that federal marshal arrest Mister Donavon for interferin' in your affairs, an' the affairs of the Bannock . . . You better do it."

Revelton looked steadily at Gus for a moment, then looked at Macdonald who was showing a humourless little wolfish smile.

Revelton twisted to look at one of his companions from the reservation. That man, thin-faced and weathered to the colour of copper, had an amused, ironic look on his face. Revelton said, "Ambrose . . . ?"

The aide swung his attention from Gus to Revelton. "It'll take some pondering, Mister Revelton. We'd ought to go back and explain things to the colonel."

Gus smiled at the speaker. "You do that, friend. Meanwhile we're goin' to drift those cattle in the middle ground. Someone might remind Mister Donavon what happens when a herd of cattle stampede."

The reservation civilians rode back slowly, discussing something with considerable heat as they rode. The Shoshoni woman handed Gus a tin

241

cup of water. One-third whiskey. He drank it down without a flinch, handed back the tin cup, winked, she winked back and walked away.

Gus asked Macdonald if there were any seasoned drovers among the Bannock. He named several who had worked for him. Gus asked him to send them out to lend Art and Henry a hand, and to tell Art to make a slow drive until the cattle were between the camp and the army, then circle up and hold them there.

It was cool under the shelter, Gus sat down, asked the Shoshoni woman to awaken him if she saw anyone coming from the army's bivouac, tipped his hat over his face and went to sleep.

George Macdonald asked the woman for some medicine. She handed him the same preparation in the same cup she had handed Gus. Macdonald sighed, handed back the empty cup and spoke to the woman. "Tell these old broncos settin' here like their best friend just died, to go make darned sure no strongheart decides to see if his rifle'll reach as far as them blue-coats up the sidehill. Tell him no one is to do anythin'. Not a sound, no guns showin' just be quiet an' wait to see if this works."

The Shoshoni woman spent a moment looking at the unwashed, rumpled, beard-stubbled sleeping man. "Who is he?" she asked.

Macdonald answered thoughtfully. "Just a feller Henry met an' brought home, an' I thank the Lord he did. That's all I know . . . Go pass word around, no guns, no noise, just set down an' wait."

The sun moved, heat lingered, cattle bawled, cooking fires in the Bannock camp, which were rarely allowed to die, sent up smoke. Indians and soldiers watched a herd of cattle being driven slowly by what looked like a pair of white men and four or five Indians toward the sixty acres or so separating the two camps.

Art and the Indians penned the

cattle loosely. There was grass, no one hurrahed them, they were willing to settle down. If they hadn't tanked up earlier before riders appeared they might have been hard to hold.

The Shoshoni woman returned, Macdonald admired her. She had changed dresses, the one she was wearing now was of smoke-tanned buckskin, almost pearl-grey in colour. He saw her watching the sleeping man, watched for a while then eased back on his pallet.

Things went full circle. The difference was that when he had been the watcher, the woman had been washing her hair at a creek.

But the look was the same.

One of the old men returned. A scout had seen riders coming from the southeast. Macdonald asked if they were soldiers. The old man shook his head; maybe from that town down-country a long distance and a little eastward.

Macdonald told the Shoshoni woman

to awaken Gus, which she did by apologising for doing it even before he was sufficiently awake to know what she was saying.

Macdonald told Gus about the newcomers, guessed they might be from the nearest town, which was a good two days ride from the area where they now were. As Gus cleared his pipe the older man said, "Tell 'em it's a palaver between the In'ians and the army, that's all. No trouble, but if they come any closer there might be trouble."

Gus found his dozing horse, left the Bannock camp in the direction of the distant party of bunched-up riders. He knew none of them. They were armed to the gills, some of them even had shotguns as well as Winchesters and handguns.

Where Gus stopped, they approached at a walk. The foremost of them was tall with shoulder-length hair and a badge on his shirt. He stopped, studied Gus and said, "We're from Clarksville, a long ride from here. Word come to town that the Bannocks was on the war path, raidin' an' all, an' that the army's tryin' to catch 'em."

Gus counted eleven men. He twisted in the saddle. "You see the soldiers over yonder? You see the In'ians some distance this way? They're palavering. There's been no trouble. To my knowledge the In'ians didn't raid anyone, they was starvin', their meat allotment hadn't shown up so they went off the reservation to make meat."

The lawman leaned on his saddle swell squinting ahead. "You sure that's all, mister?"

Gus said, "Do you know George Macdonald?"

He could tell instantly, before the long-haired lawman spoke, that they knew Macdonald. The lawman nodded. "Know Mister Macdonald right well. Is he over yonder?"

"Yes. Him and that colonel from the log fort, along with the head men of the In'ians. Talkin', straightening things out."

The lawman looked at his companions. He looked hardest at one particular rider. "I told you, Micajah."

A red-faced townsman answered. "I only said what I'd heard — the Bannocks went off the reservation an' was layin' waste in all directions. I never said I *seen* any of that."

A man with a droopy walrus moustache turned his horse with disgust, swore, and without a word to his companions started on the long ride back. He was so disgusted he would not talk to his companions, not for several days after he got back where there was a saloon and other indications of civilisation, then he very slowly recovered from what he called a wild rush by idiots responding to the word of a fool and being led by a fourflusher.

As far as Gus was concerned, what no one needed right at this juncture was a band of town-riders muddying water which was already muddy.

14

A Final Solution

WHEN Gus returned that federal lawman named Greenfield was with George Macdonald in the brush shelter. As Gus approached the lawman turned slightly looking sour. They nodded, Gus got into shade, shoved back his hat and told the man on the hide pallet who the interlopers were and that they had gone back.

Greenfield listened, squinted in the direction of the distant horsemen and sighed. He knew the constable with the long hair, did not like him and was pleased he had not come to the army camp.

George Macdonald said, "Gus, the marshal here don't like what you told the In'ian agent."

Gus cocked an eyebrow. The deputy

U.S. Marshal put it plainly. "Mister, except that you ride for Mister Macdonald I don't see anythin' that's happening around here is any of your business."

Gus nodded. "I can understand you feelin' that way, but you see, I put in three years up north workin' for the army. I saw what was left when the Nez Perce came stragglin' back, sick, starved women an' kids ridin' racks of bone."

Greenfield was interested. "You were a soldier?"

"No, I was a scout at first, then when the quartermaster got sick I filled in for him until he was on his feet again."

Greenfield looked his disbelief. "A civilian scout acting as quartermaster for the army? Mister, I find that hard to believe."

Gus sat down. "Typhus went through the post. When it was past the captain commandin', the surgeon and sixty-one men was dead. The rest of us did what we had to do. I became acting quartermaster and company pot-hunter." Having said all that Gus did not smile when he also said, "Marshal, the law is the law, back east or out here. I can tell you this much from what I learned up north. When the army tries to force In'ians to fight, it's breakin' civilian law. You're the federal law, the only kind outside the army, that's got authority an' the government to back you. Marshal, that colonel over yonder's lined up to prevent the In'ians from gettin' back on their reservation. He wants a fight. The Bannocks only went off the reservation because they were starving. All they've done since going off is hunt and live in the mountains. They haven't raided, killed anyone that I know of. They haven't stole no horses — and those cattle yonder belong to them, bought and paid for from Mister Macdonald. The colonel or the In'ian agent's got the bill of sale."

Gus sat gazing at the sour-faced federal officer before finishing. "The

In'ians want to go back peaceful. The army's blockin' their path. Look up that westerly slope; see the soldiers up there where they can shoot down into the women an' children? Mister Greenfield, you tell Mister Donavon that if he don't let the In'ians pass we'll stampede the cattle right over the top of him, an' if he wants to fight with what he's got left after that, he'll lose." Gus smiled. "He knows what stampeding cattle can do to a column of soldiers . . . Mister Greenfield, if he refuses to move, you got the authority to warn him, an' if he still won't move, you got the authority to arrest him."

Marshal Greenfield had both thumbs hooked in his shellbelt as he stood staring at Gus. "Mister, you got that wrong. I can't arrest a commanding officer of the army. That's not my job. I only got authority — "

Gus stood up. "You got the authority to detain anyone violatin' federal law."

"He ain't — "

"What do you call it? Look over

there; he's rigged for a fight. If the In'ians don't start one he will. Why d'you reckon he's barrin' the path to the In'ians? Because he wants to force them to fight. Marshal, if you don't have the guts to chain him, I'll do it for you."

Greenfield had been getting angrier by the moment. His stare was icy, his jaw was set, he had high colour in his cheeks. He almost shouted when he said, "*You're* the one that's tryin' to force a fight, mister. You got these broncos all stirred up. I got authority to arrest you, an' that's what I come over to do."

Alfred Macdonald was standing just inside the shelter. His father said something in Bannock. Alfred did not draw his sidearm, he spoke harshly to the federal officer. "You'll be the one that starts the battle. You walk out of here with Gus, an' the killing will begin . . . You know who the first dead man will be?"

Now, Alfred drew his sidearm. He

let it hang at his side. There was no mistaking the look on young Macdonald's face.

For a moment Greenfield looked at Alfred then faced Gus again. His fight was not with the Macdonalds, not right now anyway. "You got these In'ians itchin' for a fight. No white man's allowed to live with In'ians. I got the right to — "

Gus interrupted. "I don't live with the Bannock. Until a few days back I'd never heard of Bannock In'ians. Mister Greenfield, if that colonel was here he'd have a fit over what I'm goin' to tell you, which is simply that General Miles's success with the Nez Perces up north set some kind of precedent for army officers. Mister Donavon is doin' exactly what Miles did, and Mister Miles got all sorts of newspaper write-ups, commendations from Washington, made himself into a hero by stoppin' the Nez Perce an' turnin' them back from reaching Canada. Your colonel over yonder wants the same kind of fame, an' he's settin' over there actin' exactly as General Miles acted. He don't give a damn about how many soldiers or In'ians he gets killed, he just wants to get famous like General Miles did. There's nothin' you can tell me about career soldiers. You go back and tell Mister Donavon what I said, an' you tell him he don't have all day to move his soldiers clear so's the In'ians can get back on their reservation. You tell him we got six hundred more cattle on the way up here. They'd ought to reach this place by afternoon. You tell him if the army ain't out of the way, we'll run close to a thousand head of cattle right over the top of him, with a few hundred fightin' warriors behind the cattle. He'll be famous . . . for gettin' what Mister Custer got."

When Gus finished speaking Marshal Greenfield's bleak stare never wavered. Alfred Macdonald jerked his head. "Your horse is waiting."

Greenfield went to his horse, swung up, looked fiercely at Gus and said,

254

"Mister, someday I'll see you in hell," Gigged his animal and rode back the way he had come sitting his saddle as stiff as a ramrod.

George Macdonald could not twist to see the marshal ride away. He looked at Gus, and grinned. "Mister Ruby, you ain't got no six hundred head of cattle comin' because there ain't that many on this part of the range."

Gus sat on an up-ended barrel and ruefully smiled. "He don't know that, Mister Macdonald . . . Somethin' I learned up north, the army used it and it worked. You tell someone the bare facts and among them you work in a lie. The folks you're tryin' to scare believe all of it because most of it is the truth an' they knew it."

Alfred holstered his weapon, turned on his heel to go among the Bannock. His father was quiet a long time during which Gus got a cupful of water. He'd talked more in the last few minutes than he'd talked in a long time. It was dry work.

When he turned back Macdonald was watching him. "You lied to him twice. You don't ride for me, but if you want a job you got one with the Macdonalds as long as you live."

Gus sat on the barrel again. "It hasn't worked yet, Mister Macdonald."

One of the Bannock elders walked into the shade. He told George Macdonald in Bannock that there was some shouting across where the bivouac was. Macdonald grinned at the old man. "Tell me when the soldiers hitch their wagons up. If they do that, we've won."

The old man changed the subject. "How do we pay you for the cattle? We don't have money."

Macdonald looked softly past the old man, out where the Shoshoni woman was standing, and said in Bannock. "Did you know my woman?"

"Yes, I knew her long before she became your woman."

"She paid me for your cattle."

The old man looked puzzled.

Macdonald brought his gaze back to him. "I have a clear vision right now of her smile. No amount of money could do that. That's full payment."

The old man understood something like that better than Gus or any other white man would have. He left the brush shelter.

Gus found some blankets and dropped flat atop them as he told Macdonald to waken him when anyone arrived from the bivouac. He was asleep in moments. Macdonald beckoned to the Shoshoni woman. She came into the shade, saw Gus sleeping and looked enquiringly at the older man. He told her as nearly as he could recollect Gus's words to the federal lawman, what had been said.

She went over, got a piece of cloth from a bucket of water, knelt beside Gus and softly wiped sweat and dust off his face. He did not move. A cannon shot might have awakened him, but nothing short of that could have.

Henry arrived on a tired horse. His

excuse to see his father was that he'd come for a fresh animal. They talked for a solid hour before Henry was ready to go back to the encircled cattle between the Bannock camp and the army's bivouac. He rode out where Art Headley was sitting in horse shade and repeated what his father had told him.

Art chewed, spat, squinted at the docile cattle and blew out a ragged sigh. "Maybe," he said. "I wouldn't bet money this idea will work. Soldiers are a contrary lot. I've known my share of them." Art paused to spray amber again before continuing. "I been wonderin' about Gus since the first time I saw him. There's a story come down here from up north about that Nez Perce face-down. The Gen'al up there made forced marches so's he could get around them Nez Perce just like Donavon done down here. The story has it that Gen'al Miles set up some wheel-guns. He meant to use them as soon as the Nez Perce come into range. The reason he didn't was because a white scout up there poured water into the barrels of them guns. The reason he done that was because he knew Gen'al Miles, like all the army, wanted bloody revenge for Gen'al Custer. He wasn't goin' to palaver, he was goin' to massacre them Nez Perce.

"He had the guns ready. When he give the command with the In'ians pretty close, the guns wouldn't go off. So he had to parley an' turn the In'ians back without gettin' revenge for Custer."

Henry looked at Art. "I never heard that story."

"You're too young. The Custer mess happened about the time you was born. As for Gen'al Miles's artillery pieces that wouldn't shoot — him an' the army in general didn't encourage the spreadin' of that story. But it spread anyway . . . Henry, I been wonderin' all day: Do you expect Gus . . . I mean, he come from up there, he worked for the army, sure as hell he knew about water bein' poured over the powder . . . "

Henry too eyed the resting cattle. "You figure to ask him, Art?"

The old rider stared. "A man don't ask other folks personal things. If your daddy didn't teach you that, I'll do it for him. You don't say anythin' to Gus about what I just told you, an' you don't ask no personal questions of any kind. Get up, boy, there's activity over in the shade of that wagon where they been palavering."

The sun had moved, the cattle had been lying comfortably chewing cuds, but Art Headley, an old hand, knew that soon now the cattle would be thirsty, which meant they would want to leave the grazed off place in search of water, and holding them would require more than two mounted men.

While Art and Henry began turning back the few cattle who would otherwise have left the circle, three mounted men rode out and around the cattle in the direction of the Bannock camp.

They were seen almost as soon as they left the bivouac. Word spread among the Indians, whose normal fatalism had just about run its course. Like people everywhere, they could live with tension just so long; they may have developed an ability to do this longer than most people, but the sight of those three riders, one in uniform, the other two civilians, brought the Bannock to an alert status.

Before the riders reached the camp the Shoshoni woman sank to her haunches beside old Macdonald's pallet with a tin cup of his 'medicine' and as he drank she said. "The soldiers are moving."

Macdonald lowered the half empty cup. He gazed at the woman. "Forming up, are they?"

She gestured. "The soldiers on the sidehill that overlooks our camp are moving."

"Closer to the camp?"

"No, they are trailing toward the bivouac." She helped him rise up enough to see the westerly hills. He watched for a few moments then as she eased him back down he said, "Wake Gus."

This time when she awakened him she pointed. Gus sat up, looked toward the west, watched blue uniforms among the stones and underbrush up there, then said, "Is Mister Macdonald awake?"

"Yes, he saw them. There are three riders coming from the army. One soldier, two civilians."

Gus stood up, spat aside, dropped his hat into place and hesitated before going over where the pallet was. He smiled at the Shoshoni woman. She arose. He leaned, swiftly kissed her cheek, then hurried across to the pallet.

She stood like a statue for a long moment, then left the brush shelter.

Macdonald nodded at Gus. "We bluffed 'em," he said.

Gus slowly shook his head. "We weren't bluffing."

Macdonald raised an arm. Three

men, one in uniform, had left their horses with the Indians and were approaching the brush shelter. One was an officer, a captain, whom Gus thought he had seen before but was not sure. The other two were the U.S. Deputy Marshal, looking as though he'd been drinking unsweetened lemon juice. The third man was that aide to the Indian agent, the sun-darkened lean man with the expression which had seemed to George to be a mixture of irony and detachment.

The officer stopped in brush-shelter shade, nodded stiffly to Macdonald, and said, "Colonel Donavon's compliments, sir, and his wishes for your speedy recovery."

Macdonald nodded without speaking. He put his attention upon the federal marshal but Greenfield remained sourly silent. The third man, the agent's aide sat on the barrel and was not at all stiff nor antagonistic. He even smiled at Macdonald. "I'll tell you for a fact, Mister Macdonald, the colonel didn't like what the marshal was told over here. He said he never intended to fight the Indians. He said — "

Macdonald interrupted with a flinty look. "Is he or ain't he goin' to get the hell out of the way so's the Bannock can go to the reservation? That's the only thing we're interested in right now. Yes or no. We can palaver later."

The federal lawman reddened, the captain looked toward the westerly sidehill where the last of the blue uniforms were already near the bivouac.

The aide's smile was fixed when he answered Macdonald. "The army's goin' to leave. Colonel Donavon said he'd go out a mile or so and watch. If there was any trouble he'd come back."

Gus and Macdonald exchanged a look before Macdonald replied to the Indian agent. "We'll stay put until he's out that far. An' as for him settin' out there, I'd say he's doin' that to keep from lookin' like the In'ians out manoeuvred him."

The captain started to protest. Gus spoke first. "If he's got to do that so's he won't lose face, fine. Just do it. Go back an' tell him to start moving."

The captain faced Gus. "He has passed the orders. We'll be moving as soon as I get back with whatever message Mister Macdonald wants me to take back to him."

Macdonald and Gus again exchanged a look before the wounded man replied to the officer. "Tell him he's doin' the right thing. Tell him I'd like to have him have supper with me any time he's got the notion. Tell him the Bannock thank him for not bein' another squaw an' pup killer in a blue suit."

The captain waited, Macdonald said no more, the officer left the shelter for his horse. The agent's aide stood up. "About who pays for those cattle. Mister Macdonald . . . "

"They're paid for. You go back and start things moving so's when those cattle are gone there'll be more. The Bannock are not your enemies. All they expect, since you reservationed them, is decent treatment. Your damned government better figure the only way can they keep peace is by keepin' its word — for a change."

After the aide left Macdonald called to the Shoshoni woman for his medicine, which she brought him with an impassive face. She watched him sip and looked at Gus, but he shook his head. All he wanted was a bath, a shave, something to eat and twenty-four hours of rest.

As she was taking back the empty cup she spoke to Gus but without taking her eyes off the man on the pallet.

"Soldiers get medals, Indians will continue to struggle for respect, their own and the respect of others . . . What will your reward be?"

Both men looked at her, neither man was educated beyond what was required from day to day. Macdonald's gaze in particular, was softer than Gus had seen since he'd met the older man.

She turned when Gus remained silent. He smiled a little at her. "I'll tell you what I think about rewards. Men work for money. They work even harder for fame, like Mister Donavon . . . There are things that need doing with no reward attached."

He left the wounded man with the Shoshoni woman, went out to watch the wagons being hitched, the soldiers being organised to march, and he saw Art Headley and Henry Macdonald watching all that preparation from horseback.

He had won. If he hadn't seen what had happened up north between the army and the Nez Perce he would never have compared the two instances, and decided to use cattle, instead of water this time, to pursue a course he knew in his heart and head was the right one.

The Indians were packing, breaking camp, the soldiers were moving away, the trail to the reservation was open, a man could only help resolve one issue at a time. Whether the government and its agent would see to it that the Bannock never again had to break out to avoid starvation, was something for someone to worry about in the future.

He went searching for his horse amid the dust, confusion and noise of the Bannock. When he found him, he set his back to the improvised brush shelter where a wounded man had visiting Bannock elders. The Shoshoni woman was not at the shelter.

Gus mounted his animal, threaded his way through the chaos of the Indian encampment, eventually worked his way to open country, lifted his horse into an easy lope in a southwesterly direction and did not look back.

If he had he might have seen the Shoshoni woman standing apart from the camp, at the farthest edge of it, watching him grow small as he covered more miles.

FIGHTING RAMROD
Charles N. Heckelmann

Most men would have cut their losses, but Frazer counted the bullets in his guns and said he'd soak the range in blood before he'd give up another inch of what was his.

LONE GUN
Eric Allen

Smoke Blackbird had been away too long. The Lequires had seized the Blackbird farm, forcing the Indians and settlers off, and no one seemed willing to fight! He had to fight alone.

THE THIRD RIDER
Barry Cord

Mel Rawlins wasn't going to let anything stand in his way. His father was murdered, his two brothers gone. Now Mel rode for vengeance.

ARIZONA DRIFTERS
W. C. Tuttle

When drifting Dutton and Lonnie Steelman decide to become partners they find that they have a common enemy in the formidable Thurston brothers.

TOMBSTONE
Matt Braun

Wells Fargo paid Luke Starbuck to outgun the silver-thieving stagecoach gang at Tombstone. Before long Luke can see the only thing bearing fruit in this eldorado will be the gallows tree.

HIGH BORDER RIDERS
Lee Floren

Buckshot McKee and Tortilla Joe cut the trail of a border tough who was running Mexican beef into Texas. They stopped the smuggler in his tracks.

BRETT RANDALL, GAMBLER
E. B. Mann

Larry Day had the choice of running away from the law or of assuming a dead man's place. No matter what he decided he was bound to end up dead.

THE GUNSHARP
William R. Cox

The Eggerleys weren't very smart. They trained their sights on Will Carney and Arizona's biggest blood bath began.

THE DEPUTY OF SAN RIANO
Lawrence A. Keating and
Al. P. Nelson

When a man fell dead from his horse, Ed Grant was spotted riding away from the scene. The deputy sheriff rode out after him and came up against everything from gunfire to dynamite.

FARGO: MASSACRE RIVER
John Benteen

The ambushers up ahead had now blocked the road. Fargo's convoy was a jumble, a perfect target for the insurgents' weapons!

SUNDANCE: DEATH IN THE LAVA
John Benteen

The Modoc's captured the wagon train and its cargo of gold. But now the halfbreed they called Sundance was going after it . . .

HARSH RECKONING
Phil Ketchum

Five years of keeping himself alive in a brutal prison had made Brand tough and careless about who he gunned down . . .

FARGO: PANAMA GOLD
John Benteen

With foreign money behind him, Buckner was going to destroy the Panama Canal before it could be completed. Fargo's job was to stop Buckner.

FARGO: THE SHARPSHOOTERS
John Benteen

The Canfield clan, thirty strong were raising hell in Texas. Fargo was tough enough to hold his own against the whole clan.

PISTOL LAW
Paul Evan Lehman

Lance Jones came back to Mustang for just one thing — revenge! Revenge on the people who had him thrown in jail.

HELL RIDERS
Steve Mensing

Wade Walker's kid brother, Duane, was locked up in the Silver City jail facing a rope at dawn. Wade was a ruthless outlaw, but he was smart, and he had vowed to have his brother out of jail before morning!

DESERT OF THE DAMNED
Nelson Nye

The law was after him for the murder of a marshal — a murder he didn't commit. Breen was after him for revenge — and Breen wouldn't stop at anything . . . blackmail, a frameup . . . or murder.

DAY OF THE COMANCHEROS
Steven C. Lawrence

Their very name struck terror into men's hearts — the Comancheros, a savage army of cutthroats who swept across Texas, leaving behind a bloodstained trail of robbery and murder.

SUNDANCE: SILENT ENEMY
John Benteen

A lone crazed Cheyenne was on a personal war path. They needed to pit one man against one crazed Indian. That man was Sundance.

LASSITER
Jack Slade

Lassiter wasn't the kind of man to listen to reason. Cross him once and he'll hold a grudge for years to come — if he let you live that long.

LAST STAGE TO GOMORRAH
Barry Cord

Jeff Carter, tough ex-riverboat gambler, now had himself a horse ranch that kept him free from gunfights and card games. Until Sturvesant of Wells Fargo showed up.

McALLISTER ON THE COMANCHE CROSSING
Matt Chisholm

The Comanche, McAllister owes them a life — and the trail is soaked with the blood of the men who had tried to outrun them before.

QUICK-TRIGGER COUNTRY
Clem Colt

Turkey Red hooked up with Curly Bill Graham's outlaw crew. But wholesale murder was out of Turk's line, so when range war flared he bucked the whole border gang alone . . .

CAMPAIGNING
Jim Miller

Ambushed on the Santa Fe trail, Sean Callahan is saved by two Indian strangers. But there'll be more lead and arrows flying before the band join Kit Carson against the Comanches.

GUNSLINGER'S RANGE
Jackson Cole

Three escaped convicts are out for revenge. They won't rest until they put a bullet through the head of the dirty snake who locked them behind bars.

RUSTLER'S TRAIL
Lee Floren

Jim Carlin knew he would have to stand up and fight because he had staked his claim right in the middle of Big Ike Outland's best grass.

THE TRUTH ABOUT SNAKE RIDGE
Marshall Grover

The troubleshooters came to San Cristobal to help the needy. For Larry and Stretch the turmoil began with a brawl and then an ambush.

WOLF DOG RANGE
Lee Floren

Will Ardery would stop at nothing, unless something stopped him first — like a bullet from Pete Manly's gun.

DEVIL'S DINERO
Marshall Grover

Plagued by remorse, a rich old reprobate hired the Texas Trouble-shooters to deliver a fortune in greenbacks to each of his victims.

GUNS OF FURY
Ernest Haycox

Dane Starr, alias Dan Smith, wanted to close the door on his past and hang up his guns, but people wouldn't let him.

DONOVAN
Elmer Kelton

Donovan was supposed to be dead. Uncle Joe Vickers had fired off both barrels of a shotgun into the vicious outlaw's face as he was escaping from jail. Now Uncle Joe had been shot — in just the same way.

CODE OF THE GUN
Gordon D. Shirreffs

MacLean came riding home, with saddle tramp written all over him, but sewn in his shirt-lining was an Arizona Ranger's star.

GAMBLER'S GUN LUCK
Brett Austen

Gamblers seldom live long. Parker was a hell of a gambler. It was his life — or his death . . .

ORPHAN'S PREFERRED
Jim Miller

Sean Callahan answers the call of the Pony Express and fights Indians and outlaws to get the mail through.

DAY OF THE BUZZARD
T. V. Olsen

All Val Penmark cared about was getting the men who killed his wife.

THE MANHUNTER
Gordon D. Shirreffs

Lee Kershaw knew that every Rurale in the territory was on the lookout for him. But the offer of $5,000 in gold to find five small pieces of leather was too good to turn down.

THE RANGE
Lee Floren

Doc Mike and the farmer stood there alone between Smith and Watson. There was this moment of still